Plaguesongs

Crowsongs

Ghostsongs

Plaguesongs

Crowsongs

Ghostsongs

JAMES OSMER

Plaguesongs Crowsongs Ghostsongs

ISBN: 979-8-218-89988-2

Contact the author at mantabass@yahoo.com

For Rudy Mochnick – a human agent of
kindness

For Rudy Blackhawk – a canine agent of
kindness

For Raphael Aloysius Lafferty – an agent of
the unfathomable

"I am alive, when the world thinks that I am dead.
That is enough for me."

Saad Z. Hossain, *Djinn City*

"These Songs are not meant to be understood, you understand.
They are only meant to terrify & comfort."

John Berryman, *Dream Song 366*

JAMES OSMER

Table of Contents

1 - Seer

"You're not really a butcher, are you?" said the naked woman to the naked man in her bed.

"Well not a good one I guess," Rudy Lafferty replies. He covers up his lower half with the sheets. She does not cover up and sits lotus style at the head of the bed. This is her room in her house.

The sheets are green silk. Somewhere between the green of endless trees in infantry formation in the taiga and the green of tangled vines of the Sargasso sea. And like both, there is movement even without wind or wave.

"You see, I only date butchers. Something about their hands, knowing where the muscles and the bones come together and releasing the tension. It can be a form of magic."

They have had time for a thorough tattoo inventory. She has animals, both mythical and possible, in various locations. A green and red dragon on her right thigh. A rainbow toucan on her left shoulder. An entire crayon box of colorful fish circling both her ankles.

He is completely free of tattoos. He also does not have any visible scars.

"You came into the shop scouting out options? That seems a bit predatory."

"Selective. I think of it as selective."

"So I am not your first butcher?"

She smiles. "You don't know if you want to know that answer. What kind of woman am I? Well, you are my eleventh butcher. There are not so many out there and they get claimed fast. Some young fragile dragonfly of a girl seems to come along and get there first."

She had gorged just as he had at dinner. Sitting across from him eating European style, never setting the knife and fork down. She was an adept artist even with a dulled restaurant steak knife. She spun it in her hand like a drummer with their sticks, like a painter with their brush. She had stared directly at him as she ate. He thought she might be a potential kidney thief. They were two legitimate carnivores at work. Two lions sharing the same zebra.

Inside her house, he had lifted her easily off her feet. His butcher secondary skills kicked in and he made a mental estimate of her weight accurate to a tenth of a pound. He did not have to correct for shoes because they had already fallen off in two thuds to the hardwood floor.

She pulls on a shirt which allows him to make eye contact. "Are you new to the butcher trade?"

"No, I've been doing this for seven years. Hopping from shop to shop. I wake up each morning and wonder why I'm doing a job that I am no good at. As if today is my first day on the job and I'm trying to fake my way through. Maybe tomorrow I will wake up as an accountant and be equally bad at that."

His mind is a bit lost in the room. It smells of peeled oranges, and it smells of bananas past ripe that are only useful in a banana bread recipe. It smells like those stores in the mall that sell lotions and body sprays and shower gels. A sensory wall that could block you from entering. Greenhouse berries and hothouse flowers. This is a fruit stand not a meat counter.

One aspect of his disorientation is that he cannot remember her name. He remembers her introduction, but the important word is blurred out. Redacted. He may have even asked for it again.

Is it one of these "A" names? Of dangerous women who can destroy and for whom men go willingly? Amber. Amanda. April.

Or a name chosen from a favorite song by parents. Eleanor. Lola. Layla. Angie.

The name is not retrievable, but he is trying and likely missing what she is saying now. An elusive name. A tinnitus chime that burrows away from the mind that seeks its origin. Tunneling further away, away.

Then Rudy understands. He knows now that she is hiding her name from him. He does not know how she is doing this or what this means. But, he is sure. This is purposeful.

Rudy scans the artwork in the room which is primarily in pastel colors. Impressionist prints. He thinks of her as Winter-waiting-for-spring. Denier of the cold outside and the calendar.

"Listen you seem like a lovely man, I could set you up with one of my friends."

"No thanks I don't need any references." He starts collecting his clothes from the floor.

Her eyes open wide with realization. "Are you in love with me already?"

He does not answer at first, which is another way of answering the question. "I would not be here if I wasn't."

"Oh, you are one of those. A throwback. I am not like that. I don't throw my heart around until I know. You shouldn't fall in love on a second date. Free advice. You won't last very long doing that."

He does not answer.

"For fun, I could tell you your fortune. I have a tarot deck," she says.

"No tarot cards. Those are scary things."

"Okay, how about a compromise? I will use a regular deck of cards. Standard pack of bicycle playing cards. You can shuffle." She takes a deck from the nightstand next to the bed. She does not wait for his answer.

She also places rings on several of her fingers, each unlike the other. They feel like weaponry and not decorative. Gauntlets. Brass knuckles. Talismans of grounding.

Rudy does not have a knack for shuffling cards. Some spill out. One card is face up and has to be re-integrated into the crowd. He cannot get to that cracking sound of the deck being correctly shuffled.

"Now the normal deck of cards and a tarot deck have some common origins. There are equivalents for each card."

"If you can tell fortunes, why not tell your own?"

"Oh, I do. Over and over again. The cards told me to find a butcher. A repeated signal. Now cut the cards and show me your card."

He shows her the card, and she twists her face sour apple style. She takes the card and tosses it face up between them on the bed.

"The ace of spades. The death card. Well not what we wanted to see. But now that is out of there, what else can we find out. It doesn't necessarily mean something grim. Let's try again."

The second card surprises her. He sees her eyes open very wide and she stares at him.

"No no no. this isn't possible. This is a single complete deck."

She grabs the second card and throws it on the bed. She exclaims "Shit" as she touches it and brings her fingers to her mouth to cool them down.

"Give me all those." She fans the entire deck in front of her face and begins to shake.

Rudy says, "What's the matter." He looks at the second ace of spades on the bed. "Are they all that card?"

"Not all but several of them are. The other cards are there to amplify or clarify. They make it more specific. They make it worse."

Without looking at them, she collects all the cards into the package and places them back into the top drawer of the nightstand. She is crying now while backing herself away from him towards the far corner of the room.

"You have to go now. You can't be here. If it finds you here it might take me too. I can't help you. You need to leave."

"You're not serious."

"I'm totally serious. Quick, get your clothes on. Don't call me. Don't try to see me."

"What is going to happen?"

She yells, "You are going to die! You are being hunted. You are being pursued. It will track you down while you sleep so you don't have much time left."

He gathers his clothes from the floor. He can only find one sock, so he does without. No socks can be presentable and properly explained, but one sock looks like mental illness.

She does not say anything more. She does not look at him again. She has seen monsters tonight. He closes the front door of her house. He hears the abrupt slamming of a bolt. The front porch light goes off. He feels the cool evening breeze on his bare ankles.

He does not listen to any music on the drive home. This neighborhood is unknown to him, so he makes a few wrong turns before finding a main road that he does know.

2 – Two and a Half Years of Solitude

There are naturally occurring structures of time that are longer than months or years, but shorter than centuries or epochs. One of these is very nearly two and a half years long.

This structure is a useful reference in the length of a plague, in the attention span of sweethearts, in the patience of a boss who inherited you. It is the amount of time it takes to fill your brain with quantum mechanics textbooks and crazy South American novels before your health fails.

Two and a half years is the toleration of a nation for war. It is more time than Lewis and Clark took to cross a continent but less time than it took Magellan to circle the globe.

Three of these is a reasonable lifespan for an American crow.

There are habits, hobbies, or obsessions your friends will tolerate for two years. But before this phase reaches three years, they will step in.

When you study time, which requires no degree but does require explicit invitation, you will spot these discreet intervals throughout history. Throughout your own life. Those that study, not as a student would but as a detective would, have noticed other seams and fine details.

There is an overlay of cities on top of each other. Your brain only lets you travel to some of them, and some combinations cannot be viewed simultaneously.

The overlay of ants, for example, will lock you out of all the others. You become a statue, a witness to the velocity of unimaginable armies. Everything that is larger seems just a static background.

The overlay of crows resides in close proximity. It is a slower spin of the skies. It requires you to pay attention. You are welcome in this world, but the doorway is made of sheet paper that will never again be restored to a barrier. You will always see the crows from here out, and they will notice you. They will scream for food. They will get trustingly close. In every scene, your first task is to locate the nearest ones. Those on the ground. Those up high. Why are there paintings with no crows in the corners?

There is also an overlay of rain though it will hibernate for a few months in the summer. The rain is ubiquitous. It does not fall hard, and it falls seemingly slow. You are not sure if it is falling or just holding its position in the air. Everything gets slightly wet, and you learn to live with it. Umbrellas are for tourists and for people from out of state. But the rain is everywhere. It is its own kingdom. It is its own food chain.

There is an overlay of spirits too. They are mistaken for angels. They are mistaken for demons. They are rounding errors. They are the finders of flaws in natural laws. They slip through. They are impossible and imaginary. They are the best parts of your favorite stories. They are the reasons some people are labeled insane.

One of these unnamed measurements of time starts now though it will be months before this is recognized. There should be an agreed upon term in the taxonomy of time. But those with the authority, who could come to an agreement at a loud table, over several rounds of drinks about a natural thing that they all agree exists have chosen to argue and delay. They choose the opportunity for more of these nights over the finality of assigning a label.

Some things and some people do not have names. Some do not want names. Some do not deserve names.

Those detectives of time do not realize they will not see each other for that same two and a half years. When they reconvene, their number will be diminished. There will be empty chairs and gaps around the table.

This one starts now. This one will be filled with solitude but also with songs.

It is not just plaguesongs and crowsongs and ghostsongs. It is also love songs and death songs and moon songs and rain songs and nurse songs and ant songs and starvation songs. Cough up a goddamn lung songs. Songs without money, songs without embraces, songs without oxygen. Songs that do not repeat in a language that you do not know. Songs that somehow come out of your mouth. Underground river songs, tall tales, crow funeral sing-alongs, blood sugar spike songs. Two and a half years of time spent writing and recording in a home studio until the album is just too damn long. You were sent a box of cassette tapes with handheld handwritten labels in sloppy cursive. You were asked to listen to all of them, and you did. Though you did not like many of them.

3 - Triangulation

Rudy parks his car near his apartment. He is recklessly put together with his shirt buttoned incorrectly. Shoes without socks. Locks of hair pointing in different directions.

He is hungry and most places nearby are closed by now. He walks to the teriyaki restaurant a block away from his apartment. The place that has only two tables for sitting as most of the business is take out. The older couple that owns this place are Korean and speak almost no English. He comes here weekly, typically ordering multiple meals so he can live off leftovers for a few days. They must think he has a family to share with.

They have a high school age grandson who works back in the kitchen. Rudy's interactions with the couple are signals and gestures. As if they were attempting to do business next to an idling jet. He will point to various items on the menu while holding up one finger. The woman will point at the number on the cash register and smile.

Tonight, she is at the counter and stares at him as he enters. She begins a stream of Korean words none of which he knows. He has never been able to learn any new language.

She points at the door, which does not need any translation to be clear what she means. He asks for an explanation. But they cannot communicate. Somehow, she gets louder and louder. There are no other customers.

The grandson comes out of the kitchen and hurdles the counter like a gymnast or a cartoon superhero. He gets in front of Rudy and says "You have to leave. Something is chasing you. She says you make it not safe."

"I've been here so many times. I don't understand what has changed."

The grandson turns to the woman and says a few sentences that Rudy cannot understand. Her response is another burst of words.

"She says nothing was after you then. You can see that she is very insistent. Very sure about this. I always trust her. So I must ask you to leave."

Rudy agrees to leave. The woman lets out a short sentence as a parting message. He looks at the younger man for translation.

"She says you will die when you next sleep."

Rudy will have to settle for something out of his cupboard. Something in a can. Chili. Soup. Beef stew.

The night is dry and clear as he walks to his place. He pulls out his cell phone and goes to Facebook. He immediately receives a direct message from a name he does not know. Letters in the wrong order.

"There you are. Stay right where you are. I will be there soon," the message reads.

The phone starts getting warm in his hand. It pulses like radar. He goes to a different social media platform. His phone makes a ripping screeching noise. A guitar patch cord plugged into a live amplifier. The metal on a spinning microwave tray announcing its presence. Hornets demonstrating their displeasure at intruders.

From far off in the west he hears a version of the same sound come back to him. The sound ricochets in the neighborhood and tapers off.

The phone is now almost too hot to handle. The plastic case becomes malleable in some places. The sound again in his hand. Different pitches, but the same instrument and again the echo finds him. Louder. Clearer. Closer.

Rudy does not wait for a third sound. He throws the phone across the street aiming for the green trash dumpster, which is conveniently open on one half.

But the phone is an unfriendly projectile, scorching his hand to prevent a good grip. His toss clanks against the side of the dumpster and skids to a stop.

The phone does not much resemble a phone anymore. Little sparks and crunching crackling noises. A campfire popping with no sense of rhythm.

A neighborhood cat approaches the phone. Scouting the interloper. Hissing with claws out and raised above like a hammer to fall.

A single flash of static electricity scares the cat away.

Rudy sits on the sidewalk curb. He's waiting to see what happens next. The phone is quiet now.

What happens next is a 1991 gray Toyota Tercel with its headlights off and no attempt of braking slams into the dumpster, crushing the phone under its wheels in the process.

His first thought is to see if the driver and any passengers in the car are all right.

Rudy runs across the street to the car. He looks through the driver's side window for the condition of the driver. The windows are very tinted. He wonders who would spend money to tint windows on a car this old. He cannot see anyone inside the car. The streetlights are not much to count on.

He does not open any of the doors and he walks back across the street.

He hears a car door open behind him. There is a moment of silence before something hits the pavement with a solid thump. A heavy boot.

Rudy turns back to look at the car. He watches the other three doors open one by one. Then he trusts his gut telling him to run. Run like his life depends on it. Run like something that is hunted, that is being stalked, that is being targeted.

Rudy ducks behind that teriyaki restaurant. Past wooden pallets and other dumpsters. Past the gazebo used as a smoking section. Through a parking lot and away away away.

He does not see any figures and he has not been followed. He gets control of his breathing and his heartrate and enters his apartment.

4 – The Butcher's Bible

A man sneaks into a library with a backpack wearing headphones that play no music. Instead, they play his own voice on a loop. A message repeated to calm him.

Stay focused. Put it on the shelf. Stay focused. Put it on the shelf…

He does not need to sneak in. The place is open for business.

He is not a thief. He takes nothing. He leaves a book on the shelf.

The book is *The Butcher's Bible*. He started with three chapters, a catalogue of the sins and crimes of the three masters of 20th century genocide: Hitler, Stalin, and Mao. This proved insufficient with omissions of note both on the cruelty scale and in pure volume.

The book has grown as he researches, as he learns. He is not a student of history. He is a patient of history. The book grows at an alarming rate, like a baby bird. You just need to add more worms.

It grows with Andrew Jackson. It grows with Pol Pot. And Oliver Cromwell. Then there was King Leopold. He wonders why he was never taught about that man in school.

No two copies of the book are the same. Each new version is thicker, heavier.

He sneaks copies in libraries, bookstores, and even those mini-library boxes where neighbors share their favorite books.

He wonders if the librarians are his enemies or his allies. He worries about detection. Do they even know about him or about this book?

Are the books smuggled out by puzzled students? This reading requires more math than you would expect.

The name of the author that shows on the spine, on the cover, and on the title page is Gideon. But that is not his real name. He has taken the name from the famous Bible found in the top-drawer of bedside nightstands in hotels.

Gideon's boss does not call him Gideon because he sees the legal name on his paycheck. Gideon's parents do not call him Gideon because they are perfectly happy with the name they put on his birth certificate. To everyone else, he is only known as Gideon.

The cover of his book is his own creation. A drawing of a man in a raven or crow plague mask wearing a long black coat. The figure is carrying a medical bag with a meat cleaver protruding from both ends. The metal blade and the wooden handle.

He sells no copies. There is no price on the cover. No barcodes and not mass produced.

The book tracks only men and does not

concern itself with the deaths from natural disasters or famine or disease. No chapters for pandemics that kill millions with cleavers that are organic. Axes that live and breathe. Mosquitoes. Ticks. Rats.

Gideon struggles with the organization of the book. Should the guilty be sequenced alphabetically, or in order of their historical birth, or by the tally of their dead? Should all new chapters just be appended to the back?

There are pages in the back like an old Bible where a family would record the names of loved ones and two important dates. That of their birth and their death. In *The Butcher's Bible* these pages are reserved for those who are not loved. Some of the names are already filled out with month, day, and year to encourage the reader on format and purpose. Some names have only one date next to them, so the reader will need to provide updates.

He prints and collates copies on his graveyard shift security guard job. His greatest skill is in the professional binding of these books.

The book is not really about butchers, which he views as a noble trade. There are no actual butchers in the book, and he knows a little bit about butchers. He rents a room to one, and he has spotted no sign of evil in Rudy Lafferty.

His housemate can sit in a quiet room entirely still in a chair for hours. A man who can do absolutely nothing for extended periods of time. An abyss-starer. A lizard caught by a sudden plummet in temperature. A man posing patiently for an extremely long exposure photograph.

Gideon vomited the first time he printed out a copy. He was disturbed by what he had created. Now the vomiting is a bit of ceremony, a tradition. The anxiety and nervous energy for the mission to deploy the latest copy.

The optimal placement of the book is an evolving experiment. The proper location in the library would seem to be the history section, but those shelves are not frequented enough to ensure discovery. There is too much traffic to place the book alongside the latest bestsellers, and it may attract a more shallow reader.

He looks over his shoulder frequently watching for librarians. He has never been caught, and he has never been confronted.

Today's location is between two novels by Gabriel García Márquez. *Autumn of the Patriarch* on one side and *The General In His Labyrinth* on the other. The book is an invasive species.

With the mission complete, he feels the nausea start to fade to be replaced by hunger.

5 - Peripheries

In an attempt to induce sleep deprivation, Rudy first tries to ingest large amounts of caffeine. He works his way through coffee, tea, sugar, sodas, and various energy drinks. The spectrum runs from face-wincing bitter to face-wincing sweet. He samples the flavors and styles like a wine tester.

A person seeking to stay awake continuously for a short period of time can make this work. College students studying for exams. Night shift workers trying to stay crisp at their machines which never tire. Long haul truck drivers who do not want to ride the rails or drift into a ditch.

Rudy has inspiration to not sleep. To not die.

For several days, he self-medicates. His bladder and his kidneys work double time. A week into this experiment, he uncovers a side effect.

He begins to see images of people in the room with him. At the edge of his vision.

Upon closer inspection or a turn of the head, they dissipate while others appear on his other flank. He sees them move like real people but does not hear them speak. Does not hear the creak of their footsteps on the floor or their weight shifting in a chair.

These lesser-known creatures of the spirit world are called peripheries. They are hiding in the twelve-ounce aluminum can you drink from. Swimming in the coffee cup you sip from. They are relentless in their attendance, and they will bring their friends. They are the blurred objects you see in fogged up glasses. They take up space on the couch.

Rudy feels like the caffeine is giving him quick twitch reflexes like a superb athlete that can hit a 100 mile an hour fastball or change direction to avoid a stampeding linebacker. In reality, he is really just jerking his head back-and-forth to stare at things that may or may not be there.

Actual noises contribute to the stream of stimuli. The settling sounds of the house as it warms in the morning and cools down the evening. Simple thermal expansion and contraction of unlike materials in conjunction. Bird feet on the roof. Mice feet in the walls. Car doors opening and slamming.

Rudy stands up in the room and a group of spirits do the same. This is not going to work. The peripheries are warnings. They are telling Rudy that he is dancing too close to the precipice. He is playing in traffic. He needs to stop.

Rudy walks to the sink to pour out his drink. Down the drain. The rest of the contents of the coffee pot follows. The two-thirds of a two-liter bottle of something carbonated and green down the sewer to underground pipes.

Rudy scans the room and notes that it has not emptied out. From all corners of the living room, faces point in his direction. He is their magnetic pole.

Standing there for several minutes and then sitting back down for several hours, his caffeine level drops. A silent room though his bladder is screaming at him. He does not close his eyes for fear of falling asleep.

He becomes better at finding a sweet spot to visually scrutinize the peripheries without making them vanish. Some of the shapes look like specific people he has known. Some are completely unknown to him. Some hide their faces.

The peripheries follow him from room to room. They follow him down the street. They are there when he cannot sleep, which is always. They are poor company. They no longer multiply but they do not leave.

There are other spirits in Tacoma.

There are those that slide under the hoods of parked cars to sleep on still warm engine blocks at night. In the morning, they slither up trees where they will reflect the sun inaccurately. You can locate the specific trees because they are free of birds and free of squirrels. Their leaves hold their green the longest before they give into the colors of autumn.

Close your eyes when you start your car before your morning commute. They do not wish to be seen in transit. You do not want to see them.

If you run a spinning fan at night while you sleep during the summer, the various mechanisms will drift and align until they find a voice. Plastic and metal parts mass produced overseas. You will hear a voice speaking, though no words can be made out. The endless monologue enters the room from beyond that wall, but that is an exterior wall. When you shut off the fan to locate the voice, the sound vanishes. It takes a few rounds of this to convince yourself that the sound is coming from the fan. A complicated effect that creates a frequency in the human vocal range, but absent of language. The spirit that has taken up residence in your fan does not know any language that you know. Its mimicry is incomplete.

It was trying to tell you that it cannot sleep either. It is a hermit crab making its home in a spinning wheel.

6 - The Tacoma Archipelago

Thirty miles south of Seattle, you will find the city of Tacoma. Give yourself an hour to make that drive. Longer during morning or evening commutes. Longer during the rainy season, which dominates eight months of the year and even longer during roadwork season which swallows much of the remaining four months.

If you time it right, near dawn or dusk, you will pass under a blanket of fellow commuters. Hundreds, no thousands of crows fly perpendicular to I-5 either dispersing in the morning to their feeding grounds and haunts in the area or funneling back to their rookeries to sleep in collective safety and warmth.

They provide the perfect backdrop to whatever music you are listening to. Orchestral pieces, free jazz, gentle folksongs, angry punk rants, or heavy guitar dirges in drop-D tuning. If you turn the music off and roll down the car window, you will think that the crows are announcing the end of the world.

The city lives in the shadow of a tremendous mountain called Rainier, but that is a new name. The older name is Tacoma or Tahoma or perhaps the right name is these two spoken simultaneously requiring two speakers in practiced tandem to pronounce it correctly. Some names are like that.

There are older names too including one that we cannot speak because our mouths are constructed the wrong way, and our ears are not dialed into that frequency, and there is no creature who speaks that language that still walks this earth to teach it to us.

People who do not live here call Tacoma the City of Destiny. The locals prefer Grit City or T-Town. This is the working class little brother of Seattle.

If you enter Tacoma from the tide flats in the east, traveling across the 21st St. bridge, you will see Saint Joseph Medical Center up on the hill. A futuristic construction with four serpentine towers rebelling against right angles. The bleached white building is lifted off the ground by supports that resemble landing gear. St. Joe's looks like a balsawood spaceship from a 1950s black-and-white low budget science fiction film. But the structure is not wood, it is white concrete. The windows of the hospital are circular portholes further announcing that it is in fact a ship. It can be seen from miles away even across the harbor from the Brown's Point neighborhood to the north.

This is the emergency hospital of the area. It is full of angels and ghosts.

The angels are the nurses and the nursing assistants and the lab techs and the x-ray techs and the orderlies and the phlebotomists and the pharmacists. Many of these people wear scrubs every day. These are people used to wearing masks. People used to washing their hands throughout the day until the hands crack and bleed. A bottle of hand lotion stowed in a drawer is as essential as air.

The ghosts come from the occasional botched surgery, the unsalvageable ER situations, or just visitors who followed the patients. The hospital's shape, a curved octagon outline, creates a centrifuge maze to collect and hold them.

The city of Tacoma is feminine, but with callous knuckles and crooked teeth. *Une Tacoma. La Tacoma. Die Tacoma.* The city will hold your hand a little too tight to indicate it is surely stronger than you. That it can carry you up a flight of stairs to share a bed or can throw you down the same flight of stairs to your doom.

There are lost rivers under the Sahara. There are people in London who spend their weekends searching for ancient rivers that have sought deeper channels underground. Those absent rivers leave some signs or residue of their ongoing existence.

There are hidden rivers under Tacoma too. Phantom rivers far below the city. There are subterranean species that are rinsed clean by the current as they hang on desperately to ensure they are not washed out to sea. We have never seen these creatures. They have strong grip.

On Pearl Street, the river does not show up on any city maps, but it follows the street in parallel. The river told them to build a road there showing a path, a natural lane.

But here, right here, in a pragmatic, but disastrous decision, they diverge and the phantom river flows to the right, that is to the east. Here is where drivers without reason, without provocation, occasionally veer into light posts and into parked cars. All the traffic signs with multicolored warnings that have been put up do not change this behavior.

When the pandemic hits Tacoma, there is a scramble played out in variation throughout the city. Small groups of people form circles of trust and accountability. They form quarantine crews and they sequester together.

The city becomes a collection of small islands, a virtual archipelago. The water rises and where you are is where you will stay. Each island will hold two or three or four people and with them their dogs and cats and more exotic pets.

You pick your crew carefully. Not everyone finds an island. Some residents go unselected as they once were during recess in elementary school for kickball or basketball or some other sport. They wade knee-deep in the shallows between the islands of the archipelago. There are no vacancies and no invitations. They are stranded and they are unsure whether to wait this out, or to lay down and give up.

The island folk and the waders agree that this is only a short-term thing. This is a month or two or three. An odd phase that will vanish before the seasons rotate.

But the angels at St. Joe's are less confident. They see oxygen tanks and refrigeration trucks. They see that the white spaceship on stilts turns away some travelers.

They brace for hell.

7 – The Electrical Method

Gideon wraps a heavy cloth around Rudy's upper left arm. He is installing a machine of his own design and homemade construction. Rudy had made a strange request, and he took this as a creative challenge.

Gideon's creation resembles the device used to measure blood pressure.

There are three knobs visible. The first offers the choices of on and off. The other two rotate from 0 to 10 clockwise.

Gideon has installed three tiny LED lights alongside the dials. He runs two lead wires down Rudy's side under his shirt to a plastic box attached to Rudy's belt. Inside the box is a 9-volt battery.

Gideon is coughing into the elbow of his own shirt sleeve. A wet, unproductive cough that becomes a background sound. A machine you eventually stop noticing.

"This should do the job, but you're not going

to like it," Gideon tells Rudy. He clicks the first knob and turns the second knob halfway through its rotation. Two of the LED lights illuminate. Both are green.

"If you start to fall asleep," Gideon continues. "Even that fuzzy daydream state before you fall asleep, this device will zap you in the bicep. It should be quiet enough to not be noticed by others. Though your eyes may give you away. The battery should last much longer than you need. Under no circumstances should you wear this more than 48 hours."

Gideon continues to fiddle with the dials. "Still not going to tell me what this is about?" He waits for an answer. "I guess not."

"I cannibalized some of the tech used in those health watches that people are wearing now. We should calibrate this to your heart rate and to your size. There is a lot of muscle we need to account for," he explains.

"Are you ready?" Gideon does not wait for the answer. The first jolt to the arm catches Rudy unprepared. He yips to the zap. He loses his train of thought for a few seconds as he recovers.

"Can you handle that?" Gideon slides tiny pins into the knobs to lock their positions. Rudy nods with his eyes closed.

"I will see you in a few days when your assignment is done. I want to see how this performs. So don't destroy it when you remove it. There is just a little Velcro on the underside. You may have to resist the urge to rip this thing off in anger."

As a final test, Rudy lets himself drop off to sleep with his housemate present. He finds it very difficult to do as his mind resists, anticipating the electric shock.

As he closes his eyes he feels like a driver, closing his eyes. Hands still on the steering wheel. Like he trusts his aim even when blind while bringing down the cleaver.

Again, he is shocked by the device. Dozens of little white stars fill his vision. While he grasps for his name and where he is, his housemate claps like a preschooler.

"Perfect. I will see you in a few days," Gideon says. "This …thing needs a name. If you think of one, let me know. I am not sure there will be much demand for this."

Rudy does not feel another electrical poke until a few hours after sundown. He finds himself struggling to keep his concentration after each episode.

He sits on the floor to gather himself.

The next day is easier. A few blasts from the contraption, but he is able to function. Gideon is not around. After a few more days, the electric shocks are predictable, almost scheduled. The changing of the guard, the punching of the time clock.

On the eighth day, Rudy starts to be concerned that he has not seen or heard his housemate since the day Gideon installed his invention on Rudy's arm.

He wonders about the efficacy of the battery. He finds a stash of 9-volt batteries in the kitchen drawer to use as replacements.

Rudy inspects the battery holder and notices that the connecting wires have come off and are no longer connected to anything.

He holds the battery in his hand like an apple or a peach, not understanding how this is possible. Then the 4:45 pm zap, as punctual as a German train for several days now, hits him and he drops the fruit.

Long before the 9:51 pm shock arrives, Rudy has removed the device, damaging much of it with frantic motions. He scrubs his arm with soap, the skin is now discolored orange and purple. His arm looks alien and unfamiliar. Something that is in an in-between state.

Then the 9:51 pm zap hits him. He swears loud enough for the neighbors to hear. Tears in his eyes.

He wanders further from the temptation to sleep after two more shocks of lower magnitude. The electric bursts hibernate, no longer needed. But he will never fall asleep again. He will never see his housemate again.

8 - Ascension

On the fifth floor of an office building

a man walks away from his cubicle

toward a window in one of those schedule gaps

a fragment of kindness

when there are no meetings

and nothing urgent is being demanded

he walks toward a window that cannot be opened

there are fewer people on the streets below

than usual

fewer people in the building

than normal

finding a parking spot this morning

was easier than it has ever been

he watches a crow

descend toward

a large puddle of standing water.

the crow keeps getting smaller and smaller

then he realizes

that he is tracking this wrong

he is watching the reflection

of a bird flying high

and away

from the puddle

it is the most beautiful thing

in the world.

he stands at the window

too long

and he misses a meeting.

9 – Fattened on Grubs

Rudy is not dead. Rudy is not dreaming. He is walking on empty sidewalks through his neighborhood. He never thought he would see his hometown of Tacoma dormant and quiet. A ghost town. People are off the streets, so Rudy can be hunted without interference, without innocent bystanders

He hears the calls of robins and chickadees. He does not hear human voices.

Near a garbage dumpster, Rudy watches a crow scoop up a three-inch French fry from a fast-food container. The crow flies up to a tree above, where it joins another crow of roughly the same size. The bird forces the food into the mouth of the second. The receiver gulps down the French fry while complaining about the method of delivery.

Then there is a conversation between the two birds. To Rudy, it sounds like two raspy voiced witches having an argument while perched high on the branches. There are no words just tones that transcend language. If you heard these sounds in the woods, you would assume the forest was haunted. You would leave the way you came with more velocity. You would warn others of the dangers. You might describe what the witch looked like.

The first crow takes off again for more food. The cartoonish, clumsy oversized baby makes demands for more.

The crows in this neighborhood have eaten well, growing fat and round. They aspire to be the size of ravens. They are fattened by the discarded waste from people and from a diet of grubs.

The European chafer beetle has spread invasively across the Pacific Northwest, colonizing parks and suburban lawns. It has taken a decade, four of those two-and-a-half-year intervals, for them to reach this part of Tacoma. The grubs are the larva stage of the beetles.

The grubs live shallow under the grass, feeding on the roots. They especially prefer the dry grass. The summer lawns that are unhealthy and neglected are their pastures.

The grubs have become a delicacy to crows who can sense them under the soil. The crows tear apart lawns to get these treats. They follow the grubs like wolves follow caribou. They grow rounder and rounder still. They discard the grass stems like the ribs of a consumed animal.

The ground looks like it has been tilled silently while homeowners slept. The crows rip out the most useless flamboyant excess of the American suburb. Prevention is simple but expensive. Proper, even excessive watering and the frequent application of fertilizer will keep the grubs out of your yard.

Neglect leads to severe lines of denounced sin which follow property lines, perfectly mimicking the surveyor maps filed with the city

The people with high water bills who have installed automated sprinkler systems look down their noses at those who have not given their lawns that attention. The destruction of a specific yard is a judgment. Enacted by an unknown culprit, an invisible punisher. Many people do not notice the presence of the crows in their midst. An unorganized army sharing their space. Most people do not know about the grubs.

To Rudy, the ravaged front yards of his neighbors are a complete mystery. Is this some odd purposeful landscaping? Is this vandalism by some unknown creatures who dig at midnight?

A large dog slowly limps in front of him on the sidewalk. He is lean with tan fur and a gray muzzle. Not on a leash.

The dog moves in a way to maintain a consistent distance between him and Rudy. He speeds up to prevent Rudy from passing but waits when Rudy stops. In this way, they move down the sidewalk in sync.

Rudy thinks the dog is trying to stay in front of him or perhaps attempting to lead him somewhere.

A young woman on a bicycle stops and waits a block ahead of them. The tail of the dog speeds up. The limping progress speeds up.

The woman has blonde, braided hair. Very tan arms stick out of a sleeveless sundress with intricate patterns of turquoise and orange and olive green.

As the dog and Rudy close the gap on the

woman, Rudy smells her wake, her cloud. Onions, and patchouli.

The back of her bike holds what looks like a gigantic bird's nest.

10 - An Unread Email to a Young Man in China

I have not heard from you in so long.

I don't know if you got sick or got in some sort of trouble.

Did your parents find out about us?

I wish you had let me come with you over the holidays.

You know there is nothing holding me here not even my job.

I know your parents would not approve.

They wanted you to come to America.

Meet a nice girl.

I'm certainly not that.

I wanted to see Beijing with you, to see Shanghai with you.

We could have pretended to just be good friends.

Everything here is strange now.

I still go to work but now the building is empty.

My roommate just stopped going to his.

He's a little freaked out and talks even less than before.

He had me build him a device to keep him from sleeping.

Where are you?

Just give me a sign that you got this email. That you are still alive.

I will fly to you.

Hell, I will swim to you.

Do you have the virus or are you mad at me?

I can only keep doing this if I know you exist.

Gideon

11 – Masks and Gloves

Rudy does his grocery shopping at night. Less crowded. People leave him alone which he prefers.

As he is walking through the automatic doors at the store entrance, a young couple is leaving. They are wearing what look like surgical masks. He thinks about the people in Japan who cover their faces when they have a cold. He thinks of cancer patients going through radiation treatment or chemotherapy. Attempting to keep out germs.

This couple give him extra space, inching away from him.

He smiles at them, but he cannot tell if they smile back. He only sees their eyes which seem to do the exact opposite of a smile.

He takes a red plastic shopping basket and starts in the meat section. He always starts in the meat section.

A woman is startled by him as he bumps into

her cart. She is also wearing a cloth mask decorated with three rhinos of unrealistic colors.

She wards him away with an outstretched hand, which is hidden by a latex glove. She hisses at him like an opossum on a backyard fence.

He bounces away from her with a mumbled apology.

There are more people, all of them masked. Even the children. There are more gloves too.

The wheels of shopping carts screech, as their drivers yank them away from him. The other shoppers give him multiple feet of room. He rumbles through the store like a shark displacing smaller fish. But the school of prey fish closes up behind him, and now he is surrounded.

A woman in bright green pajamas steps forward. He can see only her eyes.

"What are you doing? You can't be here like this."

A man with a stocking hat and a beard that hangs below his mask says, "Hey man, maybe you should just leave."

A thin younger man behind him speaks in a higher octave, "Are you trying to kill us? You are a danger to me and my kids."

Somehow, this man is also in pajamas. Then there are multiple voices. Too many instruments to make out the song. Herded by shopping carts slamming into his ankles. Latex fingers poke his ribs. The plastic basket is an ineffective shield.

He drops his basket right there. Mostly empty except for a package of bacon and a box of glazed donuts. He works his way through the crowd until he's blocked by a tall man wearing a white apron and a hairnet who has stepped out from behind the meat counter. Like Freemasons or some other secret society, butcher recognizes butcher.

The man in the apron says, "Do not bring death here, you disgrace us all."

Rudy routes himself toward the entrance. The automatic sliding doors do not open when he approaches. He is stuck there until his pursuer, the other butcher, is close enough. The second butcher triggers the door and the gate opens. Rudy leaves the noise of the mob behind.

He wonders how all of them know that he is being chased. That he is marked.

At home, he looks at himself closely in the mirror. Looking for some indicator that he has acquired.

He smells his clothes and his hands. Nothing abnormal. He has bought groceries at that same store on the way home from a day in the butcher shop. Blood and viscera under his nails. No one ever noticed that smell.

He scrubs his face and his hair. He inspects his arms and his fingers. He changes his shoes.

For a second attempt to buy food at a different store, he puts on a stocking hat and sunglasses. Long sleeves and a scarf. Again, he is singled out by a loud mob.

On the way out, the cashier throws a light blue mask at him. He catches it like a slow-moving arrow.

The mask is his entry pass at the third store. He moves amongst the witchfinders, the threat detectors, the obscured faces. Behind enemy lines. He gives wide berth to all of them. No eye contact.

There's a table covered in boxes of masks near the cash register. He buys two boxes.

12 – Your Entire Face

Everyone is more beautiful now. We can only see the top half of their face. With gloves, my hands are hidden too. You cannot see my crumbling dry skin. The severe blue veins. The spots from too much sun.

You cannot tell how old I am. If I think I love you or think that I could, I will take off my mask and my gloves. I will watch your face to see if you are pleased or disappointed.

A woman like me, who has faced years of gravity and frowns and smirks that leave creases, looks younger in a mask. I can charm you, even control you with my eyes. Eye shadow and mascara are the accents, my plumage, my lures.

You might see me bare from the waist down before you have seen me uncovered from nose to chin.

I was with a man one night who insisted on keeping the masks on. While our bodies connected in the middle, our heads scrambled to be as far apart as possible, almost in separate rooms, looking in different directions. His head rotated out to 10 o'clock and mine at 2. He will not remember what my body looked like. He will remember what my body felt like.

There are men who never learned to close their mouth when idle. Men who ask for smiles but are no good at it themselves. They are fool's gold too. I cannot easily spot them now. They can trick me with their eyes.

Has my breath always been this bad? I am drowning in this staleness. I smell like death or like something that is in fact dying. I eat mints like popcorn now. I go through several masks a day. I am burning through air filters in a pollution heavy world.

If I trust you, if I think you will not run, I will show you my entire face.

If there is lipstick on the inside surface of my mask, you will know that I was hoping for this, that I planned for this.

I want to see your entire face. Perhaps we are outside, and it is safe. Or just safer. We are not trapped in the same bubble of air, of vapor. The wind will rinse us clean.

I am not sick I just tested last week.

We are not each other's death. I want to hold your hand, your bare hand in mine.

I want your mouth, your breath, your nose, your tongue, your teeth.

13 - Sequester

The unemployed Rudy is no longer bringing in money. He spends his few reserves on purchases from hardware stores and sporting goods shops.

Several strings of mismatched Christmas lights at a greatly reduced price so many months before the holidays.

Two baseball bats from different stores to avoid suspicion.

Wind chimes and little bells which he installs inside the house attached to trip wires.

Rudy has not seen Gideon in weeks. He owes him rent money and wonders if his housemate has made the mortgage payments. Is someone paying for electricity and water?

Rudy does what he has thus far restrained himself from doing. He goes into Gideon's bedroom.

The door is decorated with a NO TRESSPASSING KEEP OUT sign more common for a teenager. The door is not locked.

Inside the room, the air is stale and unmoving. Laundry all over the floor. Loose papers on the carpet which Rudy slides on.

He has never been in here. The room is twice as big as Rudy's own room. Two corners of the room are dominated by computer desktops on heavy wooden desks.

One is bracketed by books. Mostly history books about the Congo, about Cambodia, about other countries far away. On the wall behind the computer, several postcards from locations in China are thumbtacked up. Rudy does not read the other side where the handwritten messages say standard things in English, not in Chinese characters. Miss you, wish you were here.

The computer in the diagonal opposite corner is set up for gaming. A special chair as complex as a fighter plane cockpit, various handheld controllers, a customized, colorful keyboard from Shanghai.

In the closet, he finds a pair of shoes and a pair of boots both dark colored. Nothing fancy. Long laces that need to be double tied or triple tied. The other clothing shows very little range of color. Military green, washed out gray, black, or earth tones. Just T-shirts and sweatshirts. Nothing with a collar.

The windows on two sides of the room are closed, locked and finally painted shut. Their corners are owned by house spiders big enough to scare mice. A moth flies across the room erratically avoiding Rudy's swipes and slaps. Spider temptation.

There are two empty tissue boxes on the floor. Wadded up tissues fill two small waste baskets. There is an empty package of cold medicine. All the tablets previously pushed through and out. Rudy counts four cups of tea, half filled with cold water and expended teabags. There are a matching set of black ceramic cups with some golden Chinese characters. They are pristine, likely due to gentle handwashing.

Next to the bed, he finds a book called *The Butcher's Bible* version 17. The table of contents is a list of famous people, mostly dictators. Rudy recognizes most of the names. There is an appendix with several world maps. The book has no paragraphs, just long, run-on sentences with many numbers as if in an accounting textbook. *"4,271 souls were lost, and another 2,187 bodies were broken."* The ledgers and liabilities all run to the red. The text is impenetrable. The print is small, and the margins are thin.

In a back corner of the closet, guarded by the footwear, is a metal box. Inside the box, he finds a stack of envelopes. The same ones Rudy used to pay rent with. Each envelope holds a stack of $20 bills, a full month rent amount without depletion. Each envelope is labeled with month and a year.

Rudy empties two of the envelopes into his pockets and leaves the rest. He taps on the top of the box as he closes it.

"I will replace it when we meet again. I will owe you some money and I will be glad to pay," Rudy says aloud.

He unplugs both computers and leaves the room. He attaches two metallic windchimes to the door. He hammers up three horizontal boards across the entryway

Throughout the house, he moves furniture into diagonal patterns. Sometimes in entirely random patterns. He installs a second false door to his room that presents itself to someone attempting to enter.

He paints odd striped patterns in several rooms in imitation and homage to what he once saw in a history book. Dazzle camouflage painted on navy ships to avoid targeting by confused enemies. Patchwork zebra stripes.

Rudy sets up motion detector lights throughout the house. The peripheries do not trigger the lights. He hooks up small bells at each window. He does not mow the lawn or take care of the yard.

Another week goes by and Rudy starts painting walls. He paints black arrows, the size of swords, in conflicting directions. His walls are very complicated traffic signs.

He starts painting colorful fish while sitting down facing the walls. The fish are not realistic. Some of them have happy faces and some of them are nightmares.

He does not include any other sea creatures. No squid. No crabs. No sea snakes, no whales, no turtles, no jellyfish.

The bottom eighteen inches of the house are in the ocean. When he runs out of blank space, he moves upward. He has to stand. The water level rises. The fish intermingle with the black arrows. He paints standing on a chair, trying to not repeat designs.

The peripheries watch him paint. They are silent, and do not demonstrate favor or dismay at his art.

The paint fumes fill the house, but he does not open windows. He steps outside at times and is often surprised to find whether it is day or night. He does not want to get paint on his clothes so he does his work in his underwear.

The fish higher up, those nearer the surface are better illustrated. The fins and faces have more details. But they are also meaner. More teeth. Side-eyed glances at Rudy, at the peripheries.

Breaking a three-day streak of not speaking, Rudy says, "If we had a second floor, I might draw birds. If we had a basement, I might paint demons."

He does not play music or watch television. He paints and listens for the sound of bells and wind chimes. Then the ocean is full, and he buys no more paint.

Rudy takes his efforts outside. He is on his hands and knees on the sidewalk in front of the house. He has a small brown paper bag full of thick pieces of chalk. A pinkish red piece in his hand.

Now he is making arrows and thick lines. The arrows all point away from the house or directions to go around the house. People walking their dogs ask him questions. They learn nothing useful and assume he is harmless. Elementary school kids offer to help but Rudy does not trust them to get the directions of the arrows correct.

He is not making a map or a maze. He is making dead loops and detours. He is creating confusion and misdirection. The underground rivers do not obey these new instructions. The markings are temporary, the rain will always win.

Rudy goes through all the chalk until the nubs are challenging to handle without tearing his fingernails on the sidewalk. Until the lines are dense and contradictory in color and direction. They are vertigo inducing like a man walking in a mismatched plaid outfit.

He goes back into the house empty handed.
The peripheries follow him.

14 – Pay Me in Cheeseburgers

Pay me in cheeseburgers or else pay me in cash.

Under the table under the radar no taxes no paperwork no record that I was ever here on any computer.

I can be here when you open. I can be here when you lock the doors at night or I can do both.

I will not get tired. I will not sleep on the job. Pay me in cheeseburgers. They will keep me alive. They will keep me awake.

I will wash all the dishes again and again until they know me by touch and they trust my clutch. I will mop the floors with scalding hot water that will dry so fast. I will empty the trash and reach what is high on shelves, and I will defend waitresses from drunks and angry fools.

I will not be on the phone. I will not ask anyone for their names.

If it is too early for cheeseburgers, then pay me in pancakes.

It is a barter economy. It is late empire. No one has money and perhaps this is the end of money, but we still need to eat.

I am good at listening to the ranting of cooks and the scolding of managers.

I am made of bricks and like bricks you will eventually not notice me.

I will clean the toilets. I will pick up the bottles and cigarette butts from the parking lot.

I am hungry and cheap as the best workers are. Pay me in pizza or tacos. My clothes hang loosely on my bones these days. I am shrinking but I am not sick.

Pay me in cheeseburgers or someone else will.

15 - He Kindly Stopped for Me

Tuesday morning feels like Sunday morning. All days without chopping and cleaving are alike. With his roommate missing, no sleep, and no job, the days lose structure and segmentation. When he needs to know the time, which is more rare each day, digital clocks seem like random number generators. He just has to trust them.

This is the quiet before the cars are moving, before lawnmowers and leaf blowers, before kids go to school, before the birds start singing, before construction crews make their noise.

Rudy comes home with groceries in his arms. He has been going to a small local market. Half the size of one of those attached to a gas station. No one wears masks there and they only transact in cash. The owner is old with leather skin. He grumbles and he swears under his grumbles. The store closes promptly at 5 pm as metal cage protection is brought down over the front door and the front windows.

Rudy sees a dead rat on the sidewalk two blocks from his place. No sign of violence. Not a roadkill. Just dead lying on its side.

Across the street on the opposite sidewalk, coming toward him, Rudy sees a coyote. In its teeth it holds a large tabby cat with a marble-colored coat and a fluffy tail. The cat is still and conquered. The coyote, the size of a medium sized dog, holds its head up high to display its prize and to keep it from dragging on the ground.

The coyote does not acknowledge Rudy. Does not look his way. Does not slow down. Does not speed up and does not change its path. An early morning battle of neighborhood predators. One that the tabby could have forfeited by climbing a tree or hopping a fence. The proud coyote carries the cat like a bouquet of flowers, almost too much to handle if it loses its focus. It will eat well tonight and maybe for several days. The cat might also feed a litter of pups. The coyote has eliminated a competing carnivore.

When he stands on his doorstep, he notices dents and scratches on the door. When he turns the knob, he feels it is warmer than it should be on a cool morning.

Inside the front room, he smells unfamiliar scents. It smells like wet leaves, and it smells like green. There are muddy footprints in all directions to each of the rooms. The door to the backyard is open and swinging softly. It does not look forced. Rudy tries to think if he had left this open but he never leaves doors open.

Sitting in the lawn chair facing away from the house and toward the sun is a human figure. Its hair is long and flattened out as if caught in a rainstorm recently. Its arms hang down vertically pointed towards the ground.

Rudy pauses. His heart goes into a hummingbird gear. He watches the figure who does not move. It is not alert. He thinks it has exhausted itself. Spending so much energy to get here, it needs to recharge or conserve fuel before doing what it was meant to do. Rudy does not think of it as human. The proportions are all wrong. Poorly assembled from a faded blueprint. Those arms are too long without muscle definition. They look like morning glory vines. The feet are also too long, and they lack the natural splitting into toes. The hair does not even resemble human hair, much more like moss or seaweed. This thing was not designed to sit in a chair.

He wonders if he could fight it. Kill it if necessary. It might not bleed. It might be like battling an ambulatory bush. Is it photosynthesizing even now in the sun? Is he squandering a short window of advantage? Are its battery levels rising while Rudy contemplates his plan?

Perhaps it is unkillable, a patient pursuer that will regenerate after minor losses. After all, it has the sun on its side. Rudy thinks that a butcher's cleaver, the weapon of his wages, is the perfect choice to deal with this intruder.

The figure remains silent. Rudy feels no fire of battle grow inside. So, he turns and walks on his toes to the front door. He crosses the street to where his car is parked. He checks the backseat for anything unusual, including anyone unusual.

Then he is driving down the street. He does not bother to wait for the engine to warm up.

16 - Lockdown

We ask that you leave it on the porch. Through the door, our voices are muffled. The response on the other side of the door is likewise distorted by an N95 mask. We are not yet accustomed to speaking this way. We pretend we understood what was said.

We bring in the package of food wearing latex gloves and armed with alcohol wipes. We wash our hands like obsessives, like the guilty, like nurses. This is a piece from the outside world, treasured but dangerous. We imagine a pulsing blanket of killer microbes covering the box.

We cook for ourselves and hide the box in the garage. With time it will become harmless. We kill time with the television. We watch all seven seasons of Buffy the

Vampire Slayer. We watch all episodes of Adventure Time. We slay nothing and we have no adventures. We watch old movies too. Buster Keaton, Humphrey Bogart, Vincent Price, Barbara Stanwyck, Katherine Hepburn. None of them are sick. None of them are wearing masks.

They are comfortable making contact with strangers. With friends. With lovers. Watching their unafraid proximity as a form of pornography. We are prudish while watching their boldness. We watch movies in Spanish and Russian with the subtitles off to create mystery. Uncertainty. We try to decipher the plots from their facial expressions. More faces that do not wear masks.

We forget to read books we forget to make art we forget to make love. We forget the feeling of wearing shoes for twelve hours a day. The front door is our portal to the world. An airlock with an unmeasured success rate at blocking contaminants.

We smell like the sofa. We smell like our dogs. We cry at scenes in movies where we should laugh. We have stopped watching the news. We have learned to cut our own hair. Shaving the head is even easier.

Pick your island. Pick your quarantine crew. This will end tomorrow. This will end in a decade. This will never end.

We wonder who will not make it. We look for signs of illness in each other. We poke each other at night to make sure we are still breathing.

17 - Sprinter

Rudy is driving because driving is another way of running and running is another way of not sleeping and not sleeping is another way of not dying.

He knows that he is going too fast, but he wants to be far away across town. To put distance between himself and the person sitting in his backyard. No, not a person. That thing in the backyard. He could smell it before he could see it. Soaking up solar radiation.

The first evidence in the last few months that he is still being pursued. Like the fortune teller warned. Like the woman at the teriyaki restaurant said.

He is both very awake from adrenaline and very tired from lack of sleep. He feels an electric tremor in his left arm. This is not one of those specific times of day where he previously was shocked. A misfire. The device miles from here in pieces at the bottom of a garbage can has lost its timetable but not its potency.

He has left quickly with no plan and no destination. Just away away away.

Rudy exits from the suspended concrete highway down to a fast-moving surface street. He turns the radio off so he can concentrate. He turns his head back to check his blind spot as he prepares to change lanes. The heads of two peripheries in the backseat make the same head turn.

There are fewer cars than there should be at this time of day. He has the space to slide all the way across several lanes of traffic and pull a U-turn to point the other way. He puts his hands at ten and two on the steering wheel. Sits obediently at red lights when there are no cars going the other direction.

Rudy turns his car into the right lane of a busier road which passes by hotels and restaurants and medical offices. Another car in the left lane matches his pace and drifts towards him. Gideon calls this type of drivers "leg rubbers." As if there were encroaching on your space at a shared dinner table or park bench.

He looks left to inspect, to judge, and to assess the face of the other driver. Can he safely indicate to this person to back off?

The other driver has already turned towards him. Locked in a gaze of wide-eyed intensity.

Rudy recognizes the face that he has seen so many times. The first face in his life. He sees his mother staring at him. His mother has been dead for twelve years. He was there when she passed. The version he sees staring at him now reminds him of two or three years before that last day. Before the cancer had shrunk her into nothing.

The same staring eyes, the same short, black perm, the same frown.

He focuses on the road again, trying to shake the vision out of his head. When he turns back, she is still looking directly at him, as still as a painting. She does not try to mouth words or give him any kind of signal. She is not watching where she is going, and she is too close to his car.

She has slid across the front seat and is almost in the passenger seat. Leaning towards Rudy, she keeps her left hand on the wheel, but no eyes on the road ahead. Her look of disbelief exceeds his.

He keeps his driver's side window rolled up, afraid she might leap from one vehicle to the other. She speeds up as he speeds up and slows down as he slows down. He tries this tactic multiple times, but she matches his pace like some welded metal bar has connected the two cars.

Her car drifts closer to his. Rudy braces for the sparks from two high speed objects clashing. Swords and axes on shields.

Before any collision, he pulls the steering wheel hard right down a smaller street. She does not follow. Rudy is sweating and shaking. His car gives a high shrill whistle of something that is failing and complaining.

He parks alongside an apartment complex. Getting out of the car without closing the door behind him, without removing the keys. He walks a block from the vehicle in case it is thinking of detonating. Near a parking lot shared by a pancake restaurant and a medical clinic, he sits on the curb.

Rudy stares at the sidewalk and watches the ants crawl into cracks and down the curb. There are so many. He wonders if there have always been ants on everything. He cannot remember looking at the ground while outside and not spotting their movement in just a few seconds. Ants busy with ant tasks and ant plans.

He thinks that it could not have been her. Maybe she is someone who just looks identical to his mother. There are a finite number of genetic combinations in the world. A doppelgänger of his mom might have a son that looks very much like him. She would then have been surprised to see her own son driving alongside her. Perhaps her son lives across the world and across the ocean. She would have been upset that he kept his return a secret.

Or perhaps her son is dead, and she was as disturbed as he was. A simple explanation. A highly unlikely coincidence but nothing supernatural.

He does not know what type of ant these are. Should he be careful to avoid being bitten? He read an article once about different types of ants whose territories come into conflict. At those boundaries, the tribes of ants fight endlessly. A Ragnarök pile of dead ants. The boundary shifts by a few feet with their alternating wartime successes and failures. A massacre happening at our feet, unnoticed and unmourned.

Rudy does not know how much time has passed. Twenty minutes or two hours? He has fallen into the overlay of the ants. Watching the motions of ants breaks his internal clock. This will require some recalibration.

He notices a shape crossing the road coming right toward him. The shape had once been an opossum. A creature that should not be out in the middle of the day. A devourer of ticks, a hissing shadow on top of a nighttime fence. But not a midday jay walker.

The front half of the opossum matches the field guide. *Didelphis virginiana.*

The back half has been completely flattened by the crush of automobile wheels.

The opossum is cutting diagonally across the lanes in a path pointed directly toward Rudy. The opossum ignores the incoming cars. It resists time and it resists science by pulling itself across a concrete desert. The scraping sound of its claws on the pavement is buried under the traffic noise.

A purpose, a destination. It is half of a messenger, half of a compass needle, half of a riddle.

Rudy is standing still watching the half creature. He walks a few strides to his right further from his parked car.

The opossum adjusts its angle slightly, a show of impressive geometry from an animal with poor eyesight. It does not stop. Crawling is another way of not dying. Its progress is steady and methodical.

Rudy holds out his left hand in front of him. His palm emulating a stop signal. He asks it to stop. In full sentences again and again before the words degrade into screams of "just stop." The half creature will eventually reach him even at its slow pace. There is too much day left though not much of the animal left.

The opossum does not realize that it is already dead. Rudy does not want to see this creature up close.

He runs and runs down the sidewalk. He abandons his car. He runs for blocks and blocks until his side hurts, and his feet are hot, and he is choking on dry air. He is not sure how far he has gone, but he is in an unfamiliar neighborhood. The street names are new to him. The sky is new to him.

He sits for an hour on the sidewalk. He realizes he does not have his car keys with him. He no longer remembers from which direction he came. Where his car rests.

Rudy has never been a good navigator. He did not run here on a straight line. He crossed a few streets just because the crosswalk was green in that direction. The directional choices were made for him. He followed the path of easiest and immediate escape.

Rudy cannot remember the last time he ran like that. With no brakes and with legs and feet flying. His body trying to keep up. Not thinking of the damage to his feet.

Why was the opossum coming towards him? How could it keep moving, keep breathing, keep living? It was half of itself. It was dragging and pulling not running. It was continuing to cross traffic instead of seeking a safe place to give up and die peacefully. In denial at the damage done. Half gone. A cartoon character that has run off a high cliff and will not fall so long as it does not look down. As long as it is ignorant of its altitude, it can remain suspended. It is half. But it is not zero.

This is the bottom. He thinks that he has lost everything. That he has panicked and turned into a running fool.

So much can be lost in a day. A place to live. A means of transportation. Almost everything he owns.

He has learned that he is still being chased, still pursued, still wanted.

18 – Arguing with Hungry Ghosts in the Rain

She is standing in the middle of the street in the heavy rain. How could I not go out to her?

She beckons to me with her stare, and with the motions of her hands.

My wife, my second wife, vice-grips my arm on the porch.

"You cannot go out there Samuel."

We both know she's gone five years now. I was there when they buried her.

Streetlights are just enough to identify her. I know that dress. I know that hair even though the rain has obliterated its shape.

Wise men bury their loved ones more than one night's walk from their homes. Spirits remember the way. We should have moved further away. I stopped putting flowers on her grave, when I married again.

"I can't just let her get hit by a car. Let me talk to her, whoever she may be."

Once I step off the porch into the deluge, all chances of conversation are lost. This is not a typical rainstorm for Tacoma. There is standing water beyond what the drains can handle. I am soon soaked to the ankles.

When I reach the woman, the face I see is still my first wife. The face wants to argue, wants to plead, wants to make itself known. Then her mouth is moving. I hear no words, exactly zero words.

The rain rises in volume and pitch with her expressions but there is no meaning. The face becomes two sharing the same space.

One is angry and desperate. Accusatory.

The other is soft, lost, and retreating into itself.

I try to talk, to answer, but also to listen. This is all futile as the downpour does not relent. I want to shove her out of the street onto the sidewalk, but I'm afraid to touch her. Afraid she will be solid but equally afraid that I will just pass through her shape.

I try to read lips, but I am not good at this. In the dark with two mouths moving on the same face.

She reaches out to grab my hand, but I pull back.

I am shaking and shivering. The angry face is losing momentum, running out of wind, losing the battle to control the stage. There are pauses between words now.

Then there is only one set of eyes, one nose and one mouth staring at me. It is the gentle one. The one I remember. I think that she is wearing this dress because it was always my favorite, but not hers. It reminded me of our early days, those first summer dates.

To her, the dress was a reminder of tougher times. When this was her only dress, bought at a thrift shop.

She is barefoot in the rain, but her toes are underwater so I cannot count them or see if the nails are still painted.

She gives me one more crooked smile with a canine poking below her lip. She turns away from me and walks slowly down the middle of the street.

She drags her feet. I cannot tell and do not want to know if she splashes the standing water. Like playing in the waves at the beach.

Her image dims and brightens in proximity to the line of streetlights. I can see her for further than seems reasonable.

One last fade and she is no longer there.

I return to the porch. There is no point in rushing. I am already soaked and shivering. Once inside, I pull off my clothes and throw them on the floor.

My wife, my second wife will burn these clothes. She will call a realtor tomorrow. Soon a FOR SALE is hammered into the front yard.

We will go far enough this time. Over the bridge to the Kitsap Peninsula or maybe down to Oregon or across the Cascade mountain range. More than one night's walk from a certain tombstone. We are in a drowned city walking in the shallows between islands.

19 - Corpspeak

A four-story office building rises out of an area filled with industrial parks and strip malls. It is its own hill, its own tower. Rudy is drawn to its glass doors twice as high as him stenciled with the name of a tech company that gives no indication of what it makes or does.

The parking lot could hold a hundred cars, but today it is completely empty. The small patches of grass and decorative plants have been left unattended and are branching out onto the pavement.

The front door is locked, but around the side he finds a service door meant for security and janitors that is unlocked. He pushes through dust layered cobwebs. This entrance has not been used recently.

Rudy steps inside and loses all the sounds of the outside world. He trades these noises for the hum of air conditioning. The air is moving and temperate. He finds a stairwell lit by an emergency light.

Rudy travels to the second floor. He opens the door slowly and minimizes the sound of it closing behind him.

He sees a number of low wall cubicles. From the sunlight coming in through west facing windows, he locates the light switch and flips on the overhead fluorescent lights. They buzz and hum a different song than the air conditioning. Like bees that grumble as they exit the slumber of hibernation.

Examining a cubicle, he sees there is no computer, just the loose cables and wires that once connected to one. Each of the grayish desks is the same. Under a thin coat of dust in the corner of the room, he sees the tentacles of wiring where a surveillance camera should be. In the spaces between the cube farms, he finds shelves of packaged printer paper and more cables and wires. Vacant places that once held printers or photocopiers,

He hears nothing. No voices.

He sees no one. No creatures. Except the peripheries who walk behind him and alongside him.

In the shared kitchen space, he finds plenty of dishes and glasses and plastic silverware. In the refrigerator, Rudy finds half empty pop cans, abandoned salads that have gone feral and changed their genus and species. Perhaps leaving the plant kingdom entirely behind.

The smell is overwhelming, so he slams the fridge door shut. He goes through desk drawers, and locates snacks stashed by the missing employees. Packages of cookies, cheese and crackers, granola bars, dried fruit. Sealed, and still edible. A bounty of preserved and processed food. The machine that filters drinking water produces him a cup of clean, cool water.

He inspects the third and fourth floor. They are nearly identical to the second floor. So much so, Rudy questions if he is not really on the same floor. He sticks with the stairs and does not use the elevator. The bathrooms are clean and well stocked.

On the ground floor, he avoids the front lobby area with its large glass windows, not wanting to be seen. He finds a workout room with some exercise equipment, a working shower, and two bicycles in good repair.

The walls are decorated with employee photos alongside words that once he has read, immediately vanish from his brain. They are labeled vision statements and mission statements in nonsense sequences of jargon words in bright, curvy fonts.

None of the windows on any of the floors will open. Methodically, he turns off all the lights he has previously switched on. He does not want an unexpected, illuminated window spotted at night.

He sits on the floor, his back to the wall near a stairwell on the second floor. He waits to see what the night will bring as he watches the sun set.

The large room darkens. A few exit signs remain glowing. Some dim emergency lighting but it more resembles isolated fireflies than anything substantial.

He listens carefully for potential footfalls or voices or other sounds. Office buildings have their own random acoustics equivalent to tree branches creaking or breezes traveling through their leaves.

He imagines each small sound as an intruder, a fellow invasive occupant. There are plenty of chairs to hold all of his accumulated peripheries. He is alone, but he is never alone.

He remembers every scary movie that traumatized him as a child. Vampire movies where recently buried children float outside of second story windows. He does not look out the windows. He thinks of monsters in the hallways, in the airducts. A hundred short walls to hide behind for an ambush.

In the morning, he finds no signs of monsters. No signs of anything else in the building except him. He finds no evidence of rats or mice.

Rudy takes inventory of his snacks from the various drawers. He piles his findings and then sorts them on a long table in a conference room. He notes expiration dates but then realizes he does not know the current date.

The video screen and Polycom speaker are likewise absent, leaving behind only wires and cables, like the roots left behind of a removed tree.

Once he has taken full inventory, he creates meal sized clusters in an attempt to bring variety and food group representation. Overall, this is not a nutritious hoard. While there are some beef jerky packets and granola bars, most of the table is covered with sweet and salty things.

He does not lock the door to the outside for fear of being locked out himself. He does rig up an intruder alarm. A trio of metal wrenches connected through bits of cable to the floor, which will cause multiple glasses to fall off a short shelf and shatter on a concrete floor. He is not sure how far away in the building he would be able to hear it. Would an intruder hearing this be deterred by the commotion?

On the third night he yells at the body

snatchers, at the alien invasion force, at the zombies, at the mythical monsters. He tells them to leave him alone.

The peripheries look around the room, trying to find out who he is addressing. No one responds to Rudy.

The next morning, he examines his complicated alarm. No sign of any disturbance.

He shaves and showers, using supplies he finds in the locker room. He eats three small packages of chocolate chip cookies for breakfast. He reads summaries of technical projects on the wall that make no sense to him. Diagrams that may as well be ancient cave paintings.

He eats two packages of red licorice. He looks at the framed photos that decorate the various desks. Wedding photos, baby pictures, a smiling couple on a tropical beach.

On the fifth night, he arms himself with a dozen ceramic coffee mugs. When he hears noises, he launches these grenades in their direction. Some explode on the hard floor, but others bounce on softer carpeted areas.

He is finishing up a second package of mini powdered donuts. The sugary dust gets on every surface and messes up his grip and thus his throwing accuracy. The grenades fly astray, their trajectory altered.

He is jittery in the morning. He walks out the front door of the building. He leaves the building and does not return.

20 – God's Power Supply Silent Pub

Rudy walks off a suburban path and finds a concrete shelter of three thick solid walls with the fourth side completely open to the night air. The roof is another flat slab. A homemade sign painted with purple lettering on cardboard says *God's Power Supply Silent Pub*.

There are small and low to the ground tables in each corner of the place plus a few more tables in the middle. These tables are a few feet apart each lit by a solitary candle. Next to all but two of the tables, a person sits on the floor. A half-full glass of some dark liquid rests on these tables within arm's reach. The remaining two tables are not taken.

The candles do not provide much light, so Rudy moves carefully to an empty table. He sits directly on the dry ground. He waits and looks around.

Someone walks to his table carrying a pitcher of beer. Despite the poor light and most of her face being covered by a mask, he is mostly sure it is a woman.

She fills the glass on his table with some dark beer that does not let the candlelight through.

He reaches out to take the glass, but her left hand moves faster than his to grab him by the wrist.

He looks up at her face. Her eyes are framed by eyeshadow and dark eyebrows that rise in an unnatural arc. She holds three fingers in front of her face.

Rudy digs through his pockets and pulls out two bills. He brings them close to the candlelight to determine their denomination. A one and a five. He hands both to her and shrugs in an apology.

She nods and slides the two bills into a jacket pocket. She leaves and returns with a second glass, which she also fills. She leaves him alone.

Rudy works through the two glasses. He nurses them over a two-hour period. The beer is warm and flat, and it does the job.

The other people at other tables do not speak. The candlelight does not extend into the night. He hears soft rain and then it is quiet and then the rain again.

A few times, someone gets up and goes behind the structure. He then hears them pissing against the solid wall.

At times, he thinks he hears frogs or crickets giving away their location to predators, calling for mates, or just singing in the dark. One candle burns all the way down and is replaced by the woman who carries the pitcher. The candles are votive, but they are not scented.

People leave. A new person shows up. The only vocal sounds they make are coughs and burps and sneezes. No one at the other tables acknowledges Rudy.

Rudy thinks that maybe he is in reality a full continent away. That he has shuffled across an ocean to be in this place. That there is a silence here because maybe English is not spoken here. That it is poorly lit here so that he cannot see such different faces, different hairstyles, and the clothes from that other continent. That this place is a sitting substitution for a bread line.

People are not drinking to forget but to fill some space in their stomach. Liquid calories.

Off stage or off camera, the woman pours mismatched beers from a variety of cans and bottles into the pitcher which she stirs with a long wooden spoon. Like she is making a batch of lemonade on a summer day.

But the end result in the container is not homogeneous. It is the glacier melt from Mount Rainier flowing down the Puyallup River into Commencement Bay. Refusing to mix with the water that is already there.

If you hold a pint up to the light, some really substantial light, you might see that the battle is ongoing. The laws of equilibrium have forced the different beers into motion and into conflict. The drink is not warm because of lack of refrigeration, but because of the kinetic energy. It looks like something that is not done living. Something that should not be consumed yet.

It is terrible beer, a bastard goulash, a stew that fights in your throat. It is trouble and peace dancing apart, but close in the same small room. Yet everyone here will drink until their cash in pocket goes below three dollars, and they have nothing to put on the table.

They are thousands of miles away from any place that has lockdown laws. This is a jungle, a desert, a gulag, an outpost on the edge of the wilderness or at the end of time.

The edge of the pub where the final wall would be is lined with peppermint spray. It smells like Christmas candy, and it smells like mouthwash. This perimeter attempts to keep the ants out, like a pentagram that must be painted properly to protect the patrons from demons.

Someone on the other side of the shelter offers to pay the woman who carries the pitcher with oral sex. Offering a face pushed between thighs, but she shuts this down.

"I am not that kind of girl. And the money would flow the other way. And three dollars? Is that how cheap you think I am? Get out find some blackberries on your way home to keep from starving. Don't step on the peppermint line. Come back when you have three dollars."

When the silence is broken, Rudy hears the brief conversation. It is just whispers a few feet away. It does not even sound like words, just frustration and desperation.

Rudy has taken too long to drink the second beer, so some tiny flying insects have drowned themselves on the surface. He uses the candle to spot them and then fish them out with his fingers. He then covers his glass until he has emptied it.

He nearly walks into a man on the path as he leaves. There is no apology or pardon me. Just two hands extended to create separation without breaking stride. Rudy is never able to find this place again, looking both during the day and during the night.

21- A Room Across Town

Rudy is drawn to another empty place but not by his nose. A gut feeling, an instinct, guides him to this place. He lifts the doormat and finds the poorly hidden key there. He is not surprised to find it though he has never been here before. Not a free-standing house but a ground floor apartment with only one bedroom.

When he steps inside, he feels lighter. As if he has shed something coming in.

The front room has a large faded green couch that expels clouds of dust when patted. There is also a coffee table. An older television, tube style.

The bedroom is empty with no furniture. No clothes in the closet.

The bathroom is clean. Several packages of toilet paper. Basics like toothpaste, toothbrush, deodorant, bars of soap by the sink.

The refrigerator and cupboard both hold some food, but primarily snacks. Cheese and crackers, cookies, candy, potato chips and pretzels. Rudy samples a few but he stays away from the sweets.

The electricity is on. The place is heated and so is the water. Someone is paying these bills. He takes a hot shower, but there are no large towels, just a hand towel by the bathroom sink.

He opens one of two bottles of root beer tucked in the back corner of the fridge.

There is a small bookshelf with less than a dozen books. All with bent corners and creased spines from multiple rereads. Some Agatha Christie mysteries. Some Tom Clancy novels. He chooses a John le Carré spy novel.

He centers himself on the couch. The particles he kicks up sparkle in the low angle sunlight coming through the kitchen blinds. Indoor fireflies, or the stirring of something has already been leveled.

The le Carré novel is complicated. He wishes he had some paper and pencils to take notes, draw figures, and map the connected characters. He gets confused and thumbs back an entire chapter to glean more from a critical scene. Rudy continues to read for hours though he cannot summarize the plot or explain the allegiances and betrayals.

In the late afternoon there is a fumbling at the door before it opens.

The person who opened the door stops moving when he sees Rudy sitting on the couch..

Both men hold their positions making quiet assessments. The man at the door has one foot in the apartment and one foot out, noncommittal.

He is wearing a light windbreaker with a Seattle Mariners T-shirt, and jeans that are in good repair. The new arrival is a few years older than Rudy. Some hairline recession and streaks of gray in what remains. He has acquired a jawline to his round face by ways of a thin beard. He is carrying food.

Rudy calmly says, "I am sorry. I thought this place might be empty." He waves his arm. "It didn't look like anyone was living here or sleeping here."

Rudy stands up from the sofa and an aura of dust particles rises with him.

"Sit back down," the newcomer says. "How did you get in?"

"The key under the doormat."

The man in the doorway does not say anything for two whole minutes though his face contorts and for half of that time he stares at the ceiling.

"Okay, maybe you can stay for a little while. Might be nice to have some company. The kind that you can converse with."

He introduces himself as Roscoe though it is not clear if it is his first name or last name or nickname or a spontaneous alias.

He has brought fast food. He keeps a cheeseburger for himself but gives Rudy the French fries.

Roscoe does not ask many questions beyond Rudy's name. He does claim the center section of the three-person couch.

"When the sun goes down, you're gonna have to sit on the floor," Roscoe tells Rudy.

Just before 7 pm. Roscoe turns on the television. He does not change the channel. Alex Trebek is hosting Jeopardy.

Roscoe faces the television but does not seem interested in watching.

Rudy does pay attention although none of the

categories are good choices for him. Literature, World War II, European cities, country music.

The sun goes down and the room changes. Rudy feels like it is getting more crowded but not from his peripheries. He realizes that he has not seen any of them since he entered this apartment. They have not followed him in either by choice or by some means of prevention.

There are faint lights that are not from the overhead fixtures or from standing lamps. Roscoe is flanked on each side by an amorphous glow. The shapes do not fully solidify, and they flicker like candles.

The shapes become people. A man on the left and a woman on the right. They are both very old. They only watch the television screen. They do not notice Rudy and do not interact with Roscoe.

"Roscoe, who are they?" Rudy asks.

Roscoe shows a pleased smile and turns to Rudy. "So you can see them too. No one else can. Not even my wife. Sure, she knows they're there. She can feel their presence. Makes her sick. Like nauseous, throw up kind of sick."

Roscoe passes a hand through the old man which meets no resistance. "These are my parents. Gone two years now. He passed away about two months after cancer took her. I guess they were that connected."

"But they're not done with me. Apparently, this is what they want. To watch game shows with me for a few hours every night. They don't mind repeats which this channel shows 24-7."

"So. This isn't my main house. My wife and I live a few miles out. She can't be around them. That getting sick and all that. Couldn't live like that. So we moved several times, but they always followed. Then I figured out a trick, a trap. Renting this little room across town where they can see me and I can appease them. After a few hours each night they fade out. Really, I can see them getting fainter and fainter. Then I head home where my wife is waiting. It's worked well for eight months. Better than a divorce, a lot cheaper than a divorce. Just a strange routine to get used to."

"Older things seem to anchor them. Doesn't have to be things they previously owned. Most of what you see here came from garage sales or Goodwill."

Rudy tries not to stare, but the game show seems less interesting to him now. The dead parents behave like a short loop of film. The mom grimaces and grits her teeth in a move that repeats and repeats. The orange headscarf does not well hide her nearly bald head. Her eyes are locked forward, persistent. Her shape loses crispness, like being obscured by a sideways arctic wind that tightens her face and hardens her eyes.

The dead father follows a slightly longer loop of film. His head rotates slightly to take in the room with his eyes changing perspective multiple times. Maybe a ten second loop of film. Even with his scan, he does not acknowledge Roscoe or Rudy.

"They must've changed up their programming. I don't know this one. It looks much older, the Joker's Wild," Roscoe says.

Roscoe says, "Strange that you can see them too. Did you know them?"

"No, they are strangers to me. But they are not my first ghosts."

The parents do begin to fade. Rudy can notice them becoming more and more transparent. All the colors washed out. The arctic breeze is winning and diminishing their presence.

By 10 pm, he can see no signs of the parents. Roscoe stands up and turns off the television and collects his keys.

"Time to head home. Hopefully she's still waiting up for me."

"What about me?" Rudy asks.

"I'm good with you staying here. Maybe we'll give it a try for a day or two. But no breaking things. No drugs. No bringing in other people. Tomorrow, I'll bring enough pizza for both of us. Sleep well, Rudy."

But Rudy will not sleep. He keeps reading the le Carré book though he is getting hopelessly confused. Has this writer even decided who the bad guys and the good guys even are? He gives up on the novel and moves onto an Agatha Christie mystery. He does not guess the murderer prior to the big reveal. He does not quite believe the big reveal. Does this all make sense to anyone?

Roscoe arrives just after 5 pm with two pizzas. He encourages Rudy to eat as much as he wants. To build up strength.

More Jeopardy but also Wheel of Fortune and The Price is Right. Rudy recognizes them from his childhood. The commercials are old too. Products that cannot exist anymore. Actors who must be retired by now and their silly catchphrases. Phone numbers that have not had anyone waiting to take your order in years.

As predictable as the TV schedule the ghost parents vanish, followed by Roscoe departing.

An hour later, Rudy turns the television back on. An old episode of Family Feud with Richard Dawson negotiating kisses from all the women.

Rudy focuses on the screen while centered on the couch. He calms his breathing and folds his hands in his lap. His feet are flat on the floor.

The images are now on either side of him. The same loops of film playing endlessly.

Rudy asks, "Would you like to go?"

The old woman turns toward him making eye contact. She flickers in and out. She nods twice to him.

Then the old man breaks his loop. He closes his eyes for the first time in years. Silently, he mouths a "yes."

Rudy stocks up a bag with food. He does not take any of the books.

On the coffee table, he leaves a handwritten note.

"*They are now free. You are now free. This place is no longer necessary. -- Rudy.*"

22 - Two Acts of Rebellion

Smokers gotta smoke and for the most part, we cannot do this inside except for in our own homes.

The old timers speak of golden days in the past where you could smoke in restaurants and office buildings and airplanes. Even the goddamn hospitals.

Now the smokers emerge and lean against the external walls and alleys. We rotate in ten-minute shifts, replaced by a different smoker. The social connection has vanished.

Now it is like guard duty where a single soldier is all that is allowed. We salute with our cigarettes from across the street acknowledging the affiliation.

Those vaping kids are screwing up the scent. Even with my insensitive nose, I can barely stand these fruity smells and do not get me started on the pot smokers. An army of skunks unleashed on the city.

Let me have these few feet of wall for a few minutes in peace.

I could handle the rain when we could all handle the rain. We held small torches in our lips, and we were not cold for those few minutes.

My old boss said that men smoke to look cool while they are idle and to not look dangerous. He also said that women smoke to stay thin. I don't think he knew what he was talking about.

I remove my mask, and I am free for a few minutes. Two acts of rebellion chained together.

There are fewer of us than there were a few months ago. The guard duty rotation list has gotten shorter. Sometimes there is no one to wave at across the street.

My hack and cough have a rhythm, a fingerprint cadence, a distinct voicing. It identifies me like a unique species of bird. A blind man could have known who was outside sharing the wall with him. We all have audio signatures. We can find each other in the dark.

To let loose a good cough these days draws immediate attention from your coworkers. They want to send me home. Without pay of course.

Oh, this is nothing. I had pneumonia a few years ago.

We fought with swords and daggers, and you see who is still here.

This pansy ass plague is not going to get the better of me.

23 – Six Poets

Rudy walks through a quiet neighborhood. Late morning, and no signs of people. Only the calls of seagulls and crows overhead.

He orients himself to set a trajectory for Sixth Avenue. He should be able to hear the traffic and smell the cooking from the variety of restaurants. But his ears and nose give him no information.

A small graveyard blocks his path. The lawn is freshly mowed. A man being chased as he is being chased should not tempt his pursuer by crossing here.

The church next door is the better option. He has been inside this church before. A wedding service or a funeral. Knowing no one there except the young woman seated next to him that had asked him here. He had said congratulations or sorry for your loss or something. Some combination of the two multiple times that day.

He had held her hand in the pews. She had

grasped for his while verses were being read. The precision of the words was lost in the high ceiling. It could have just as easily been in French or Japanese as in English. She had looked up into his face while the minister spoke. Looking for anything, looking for a reaction.

He cannot remember her name, just her dark eyes.

Rudy hops a short gate landing gracefully, but with a loud thump on a stone path. He passes through a narrow corridor into an outside courtyard open to the sky. He finds a circle of sleeping bags and other makeshift barriers against the cold and the rain. Shapes wriggle out of the sleeping bags, disturbed by his noisy arrival. A wagon wheel of squirming life resolves itself into six men.

There are beards and stocking caps and fogged up glasses. Patchwork clothes with each man displaying his own pallete of preferential colors.

The men are between him and the exit corridor opposite the one he entered. A way to Sixth Avenue. A main drag of Tacoma.

The six men create a two-level formation. An infield and an outfield with Rudy at the plate.

"Hello gentlemen. How are you doing this morning?" Rudy asks.

The men do not respond with words. They grunt and wheeze. Wet nostrils, and liquid-filled lungs.

Rudy notices the two men drifting behind him, cutting off his retreat. The way he had entered is blocked.

The first man, the man in the middle of the front line approaches Rudy. He is bald and thin. His layers of baggy clothes, flannel and sweatshirts, move less than he does. His black trousers with purple pinstripes are torn at the left knee.

"Why are you here? Are you like us? You seem healthy. Clean. Do you have a warm place where you roost?" the first man asks.

Rudy is aware that he has nothing in his pockets. No money. No food. Nothing to appease those that block his way. Nothing to offer as payment or distraction. Nothing to use for self-defense.

"I was just walking through. I did not know this place was in use. I will just see myself out."

The first man reaches out and grabs Rudy by the front of his shirt. He says,

"We rode in on horses that we bred with wolves.
We are creatures of smoke and wind.
No fossils or no ashes show where we've been.
It takes concentration to maintain our composition."

The voice is low and strong. A baritone with echoes of Johnny Cash and Gregory Peck, but full of moisture. It mists Rudy's face with horizontal precipitation. Rudy tries to break the grip, but two of the other men restrain his arms.

The first man speaks again,

" We are bivouacked outside of castle and keep
with no promise of useful weapons or divine assistance
or even of another day.
We are only offered a chance to serve,
out here amongst the wandering monsters.
Defending this passage cleaved through God's house.
You and your pale army are not welcome here."

Rudy turns his head to see behind him where several peripheries flickering in the daylight offer no help. One of them looks down at its poorly defined shoes. Another scans the scene, searching without success for the army just mentioned.

The man holding Rudy's left arm in a vice grip is a quilt of red material. Scarves and bandannas and ribbons.

This second man says more loudly than the first with an accent composed of whiskey and cigarettes,

"O revenants. O psychopomps.
Those who carry coins, ancient and unspendable in their teeth.
They are still a good value for barter
during negotiations on the crowded dock.
Your hands are still free
so you can grapple and force a way, the wrong way, against the current.
O ferrymen. O delinquent employees of oblivion.
You are late and you have forgotten protocol.
There will be unimpressive excuses and explanations.
Blame to be swallowed, sour and wriggling.
You think you are a swordsman, but you are really just a sword."

The third man, wrapped around Rudy's right arm whispers in his ear,

"There has been a judgment.
Mankind, once the apex of God's creations,
through his many transgressions and squandering of the garden,
has seen the Lord's favor turned elsewhere.
This is late empire.
I realize now that the inheritors of this world are already here.

Already living in our midst.
Awaiting our descent, our collapse.
They will clean our bones and nest in our ruins.
Their descendants will puzzle over the remnants of our technology.
They will be archaeologists, and we will be the history.
We will be categorized as mythology.
I suspect they will never be able to read our books, including the Good Book.
I do not grovel to my maker and beg for redemption or elevation.
I am grateful to be here during the transition.
To watch a new world being salvaged from the old.
To evaluate the contenders like a horse race.
I no longer speak of sin. I realize it is no longer relevant.
The next tenants of this world will not have this concept at all."

This third man speaks like an orator or a professor. Perhaps a preacher who is moved from the warmth of inside to the chill of the outside air.

These men are not strong. They are wobbly on their feet, poorly balanced. Undernourished. He wants to free himself without harming them.

The three men further away begin charging towards the struggle. Rudy jerks his left shoulder hard, and then down dislodging the second man. His free hand catches the first man by the collar and uses him as a blunt object to knock away the third man. Butcher's muscles.

He lowers the stunned first man to the ground like he is made of fine crystal. He says, "I am so sorry."

Rudy rushes towards the other three, choosing to intersect with the one in the middle. They collide with a double exhale of wind. Two almost equal forces.

This fourth man in the middle has a bright

floral short coat, likely intended for a young girl. The coat rides high on him because he carries his weight in the middle. His boots are painted with sunflowers and tulips. The fourth man drops to his knees, begins to cough. The cough goes on and on as he tries to regain control of his breathing. All the participants in the melee pause and wait for him to recover. As if someone has called time out.

From his knees, this fourth man in the short coat speaks,

"No one expects to walk down from the gallows.
A change in fate.
Someone changes their mind.
If this happens to you, part of you is grateful
And part of you is not.
Your benefactor, the person who changed their mind,
Wants to be friends.
You shake hands uneasily.
Not all of you came down those steps.
Your trust, your decorum, your restraint,
Are all swinging up there."

There are a few seconds of quiet and peace which is interrupted by the fifth man crashing into Rudy from his left side. The momentum knocks him to the hard courtyard stones. Rudy's right elbow and right knee take the impact. His skin tears.

The fifth man is all in black. Not faded black. Not navy blue passing as black. His eyes are wide and nearly colorless. He attacks the sprawled-out Rudy with long jagged fingernails. Rudy's shirt sleeves are torn from him then there is no shirt at all. He hears ripping sounds from his pants, but he cannot see the damage.

This fifth man repeats the same words in a loop, each time reducing the volume.

"There is a fist in a drawer
I used to shake in the air.
There is a dent in my skull
And the water puddles there."

The sixth man rests on Rudy's chest. Knees and palms holding him down as the other men join the battle. This man wears a suit, or more accurately, a combination of parts of different suits. He tells Rudy,

"There was once a useless kingdom that was full of useless people.
And the ground was bad so it was useless too. You could not grow crops there.
Cattle did not grow big and strong there.
The people were not wise or brave or very talented, but they had one thing.
They had a king and this king dreamed.
Marvelous dreams.
And when he shared them, and he told people of them,
those dreams could be purchased by other kingdoms for a good amount of gold.
In this way, the king of this useless kingdom protected and provided for his people.
He thought not much of this because when he told the dream,
and he sold the dream, then he immediately forgot the dream
and it was gone forever.
Then one day, he had a beautiful dream.
He was under full trees, unlike the trees in his kingdom.
He was talking to a beautiful woman, unlike those in his kingdom,

and it was wonderful.
They were eating fine food,
and there were birds, and there were animals of the forest to be seen.
The weather was perfect and there was nothing to make you sneeze or cry.
He had a selfish moment where he decided
this dream was not one he could give away.
Not one that he could sell and lose forever.
When the day came for the next auction in the marketplace,
the ambassadors from other countries came to buy his dreams.
He knew as he tried to tell fragments of this dream to entice the buyers,
it would slip away from his memory.
And so he steered away from telling the truth,
and he told the opposite, the exact opposite of his dream
which was full of brutality and cruelty. And terrible, terrible things.
When he told us that dream, for I was there that day,
the room got quiet in the front, but not so in the back of the crowd.
There were men there that did not look like men.
They had extra-long teeth, and their faces were without joy.
They looked like monsters, and they were excited.
They sought to buy this dream.
They asked how much and when he told him how much
and there were no other bidders.
They paid him twice as much as he asked.
They took this dream, this cruel dream, this dream of warfare and destruction,
and they made it their life and their world,
and they made it into our world."

Rudy feels the loosening and the untying of his shoes. The left shoe is rotated off his foot. The sixth man clocks him on the side of the head twice.

He feels the cold air all over. Part of his mind wants to surrender, to lose consciousness. But if he fades if he sleeps, he will never wake up. The fifth man with his claws will have shredded him into pieces.

Then the second shoe is gone followed by both socks.

As Rudy's mind fades, he waits for and anticipates the shock in his left arm. For the electricity from some drained distant battery to jar him awake. To save him, and potentially to startle those that hold him down.

So he waits, but nothing happens. There are no volts and no amps. There is no discharge to bring him back. Nothing to shake loose his holders. When it is nearly too late, he decides he must do this himself. He thinks of an elephant shaking off lions. Starving lions, weak thinned-out lions, and he is that elephant.

Rudy erupts and pushes the weight off his chest. The sixth man launches into the man with the fingernails. Rudy kicks out both of his feet to gain some room. He rolls to his right to get back to his feet. He locates all of his attackers. Two are still standing and four lie on the ground, rubbing spots that are sore or broken.

Rudy takes inventory of himself. He has lost all his clothes. Completely naked. He is bleeding from multiple wounds and cuts and tears. But nothing broken. He tests both of his arms and both of his legs. Everything still works.

The fourth man in the floral coat faces him with one shoulder drooped low. He says,

*"We are at the point of this discussion
where we will just disagree and throw shoes."*

Rudy puts his hands in front of his face to ward off any flying footwear. No shoes are thrown. He looks at the speaker, who unlike Rudy, still has shoes on his feet. Rudy looks at him in the face, hoping for an explanation.

Then the fourth man says,

"Here comes the whole fucking moon."

He charges toward Rudy, but he is more donkey than elephant. He is neither swift nor powerful.

Rudy is already crouched and in a defensive position. When the man is close enough, he ducks down further. He gets under the fourth man with his shoulder and launches him skyward. He is unsure if the moon is in that direction.

Rudy runs toward his exit. He steps through the perimeter of the wheel of sleeping bags. His bare foot snags something solid and kicks it. The object tumbles until it stops by the legs of a stone bench. A four-foot-long piece of wood. A handle of some sort. Shovel pick broom mop. He collects the piece of wood and holds it like a baseball bat. Like a weapon.

Two of the men approach. Rudy is swinging the stick. A high-flying scythe. The rotor of a helicopter.

He is a butcher who has lost his ability to differentiate species. He swings wild but strong. Then there is a crack as the stick meets skull. Poet number three is down. No more will he rant about God's judgement today. When he wakes up, it will be a different day entirely.

The others back away. The sick men with no sick beds. Wheezing and hunching over. Bruised and sore. To give the butcher some room.

Only the first man steps toward Rudy and grabs his bare shoulder. He says,

"You don't have to be dead to leave a ghost on someone."

An outburst into Rudy's face. The bell end of the tuba. He struggles to get free, but his leverage is poor and he does not want to hit the man with the stick.

"You don't have to be dead to leave a ghost on someone,"

The first man says again. Too loud so Rudy's brain loses its place. He is disoriented.

The man recharges and starts to exclaim the same phrase for a third time when Rudy interrupts. "You said that already." He grits his teeth, "Can you say anything else?"

The first poet keeps his hold on Rudy, but his eyes look lost and far away. Like a computer slowly rebooting.

He speaks softer at an even pace,

"I had an unnecessary job solving imaginary problems.
The only thing that was real was what I went home to at the end of the day.
I worked in spreadsheets. Forecast calculations that only existed to fill time.
Bastardizations of math.

In the morning, I climbed into the fuselage of my car.
A small space that restrained my knees and my elbows.
An hour of that and then I was in a tiny cubicle.
Dress shirts and overdriven air conditioning.
A cage transfer into the cubicle at the start of the day
and another one when I got into my car to go home.
Moved from one claustrophobic space to another by protocols
repeated daily.
My goal was just to survive the day.
Then there was nothing to go home to.
Then it was better to be under the sky all day.
Alone among strangers who were also alone."

The first man slides off Rudy, releasing him. He melts into a horizontal shape on the hard stones. He folds his arms across his chest, squeezes his eyes shut, and grits his teeth.

Rudy leaves the courtyard through the passageway. He hangs onto the stick as he emerges onto Sixth Avenue. Naked and bleeding.

He does not see, for he is looking forward and the six poets do not see, for their eyes are either closed or pointed at the sun. None of them see the line of faint flickering shapes behind Rudy queuing single file to pass through that corridor. None of the poets follow the peripheries.

24 – The Poetry of Sickness

The speaking of verse as a symptom and as an indicator of deep infection. Of immunity system failure.

The multiplication of poets, like rabbits in the absence of a predator, like dandelions in the absence of a lawnmower, like vampires in the absence of sunlight.

The virus springs words, not from your creation or your recollection of something you once read. Rather it is an offering. A poor value for your precious breath. It is magic beans.

This phenomenon does not appear in any medical journal articles. It is too strange and unexplainable. No one wants to put their reputation behind that. The video of old men and women in hospital beds speaking in free verse or iambic pentameter looks fake.

A nurse named Soledad in the emergency room at St. Joe's carries a small writing pad in the pocket of her scrubs. She captures these exclamations of the infected. She reverts to old skills, taking perfect verbatim notes. Using the shorthand she mastered during college lectures on biology, psychology, even calculus.

She submits these words to poetry contests and wins prizes. She receives checks mailed in envelopes postmarked from countries across the pond and from the opposite side of the equator. She uses multiple pen names as it becomes apparent that she cannot pass these off as coming from a single mind. Some of the poetry is not English or Spanish. Since the nurse does not speak these other languages, and sometimes the speaker doesn't speak the language of the poem, those poems are lost.

Another nurse in the same hospital records these on his cell phone. At home after his shift, he turns them into piano melodies. He uses a 4-track recorder to commit them to tape as instrumentals, but listeners still feel the ghost words. The things that were said. They are all about love or about death.

When he plays the fragments too many times, to carve that melody and that rhythm into his muscle memory, he ignites lust in the other tenants in his apartment building. He hears sounds of human exertion and sounds of mattress use on all sides through the walls and the floor and the ceiling. Some songs are too dangerous, too visceral, to practice more than one time through in an evening.

He is sweating which makes his fingers less accurate. One key to the left makes an errant note but note enough to break the spell. He plays the song until it needs to end. When he no longer has the accompaniment of his neighbors.

25 - This River is Missing Its Water

Rudy emerges from the passageway from the church courtyard. He steps from the sidewalk onto the road. His heels pivot as he rotates to align with Sixth Avenue. He points west towards the ocean and begins walking.

He is naked and he is torn. He bleeds from multiple scratches on his chest. As if he has lost a fight with multiple raccoons.

Some of the blood on his face is not his own. His knuckles are scratched. He has not bothered to wipe the phlegm from his cheek. Poems and rants made semi-solid. Globular.

None of the six poets follow him out of the courtyard and he does not look back.

He still carries the stick. The handle without a blade. It too is covered with a variety of fluids. Several blood types. A painter's palette stretched long.

His grip is too tight. He carries it low, like a

club, like a weighty hammer, like a burden.

Rudy walks past businesses. An Indian restaurant that should unleash several variants of curry into the air but does not. A pub that boasts about its pizza. A record store with no music playing. A thrift clothing store with no one flipping through the racks.

They are all empty. Lights off with closed signs in their windows.

He walks down the center of the road. The yellow line acts as his guide. Past parked cars. Over pieces of glass, rocks, leaves and fast-food wrappers. His bare feet do not protect him. He steps through the sharp objects, through the pain.

He does not look down. He does not notice the potholes in the road that have been half-heartedly patched by city road crews. The patches do not smooth the bumpy road but do prevent you from falling through to the underworld.

There is a realtor's office next to a place that is currently not a place at all. With boards nailed over the windows and a "for lease" sign taped to the door.

Rudy sees no one. There is no one to witness his Godiva-like journey. He should be cold, but his adrenaline still keeps his engine running hot

He breathes hard through his mouth. If there was anyone to listen, he would be heard two blocks away.

His peripheries flare up. Reflecting or feeding on the gray-white sky. On his left flank is a periphery shaped like his housemate Gideon. His thick shoulder length hair. His army surplus jacket. Those black jeans.

Gideon is a basement revolutionary. The one who can fix the ancient printing press. The one with a very custom toolbox to repair the guillotine. He usually has a lot to say, but peripheries never say anything.

Gideon is a maker, a fixer, a salvager. His periphery fluctuates and fades when Rudy stares too directly. Then he is gone.

On his right flank, a phantom imitates the fortune teller. The one who hides her name. Her full auburn movie star hair bounces as she walks. She wears a dress that flares out and ends at her knees. She wears decorated cowboy boots.

He tries to see her face clearly, but it changes each glance. He does not remember her well enough. She toggles in his memory between angel and monster. She is only a messenger. No, she is the cause, the instigator of all that has happened.

Rudy does not know there are other peripheries further out on each side. There is the woman from the car who looks like his mother. There are former coworkers and former classmates from high school. There is at least one, likely two, that look just like Rudy.

He thinks of the men who tried to prevent him from getting to this street. Were their words specific to him? Or were they just like animatronic devices, repeating their recorded lines from a speaker when you got to that spot in the amusement ride?

He carries a stick in case they follow him, but they do not follow him.

On his right a large display window holds multiple mannequins in exaggerated poses. They are wearing the clothes of the wrong season. They have been neglected for months. Rudy looks in a store display window at the mannequins arranged half like a funeral procession and half like a mad tea party.

He looks again at the image of the seer. He

watches as her cowboy boots transition into Doc Martens. She grows shorter and rounder. Her hairline rises up her back and above her neckline. The color of her hair becomes a synthetic red.

Something black and quiet and graceful flies through this periphery, and it pops like a soap bubble.

He keeps walking. The shape of the stick imprints in his palm. The wavy wood grain pattern. The flaws in the lumberman's cut.

He stops when he feels something run across his bare feet. He bends down and sees that there are hundreds, maybe thousands of ants running over his feet. Bubbling and boiling. They are liquid. They are atomic.

He sees that they have been following him. A dark trail that reaches back from where he entered the street. They are not biting him. They are not hanging onto him. They are crossing his feet, and they are sharing his path.

Rudy is lifted and seems to hover just above the ground. A playing card thickness above the pavement. He gives up control of the wheel, of the engine. A statue being re-located. A palanquin carried above the harsh earth.

He is entirely too visible He has lost everything. All his clothes, all layers of protection and disguise. He has been zeroed out. He is a mountain sized blip on the wrong radar. He cannot be here, naked in the middle of the day.

This river is missing its water. This man is missing his clothes. He is also missing the comfort of sleep.

The tiny six-legged men do not miss anything. They know where everything is. They take impeccable inventory. They cross his feet, but they do not bite and they do not climb. They are mostly going the same direction he is going.

If he is out of fuel, if he is weary, there are so many and so strong that they may be able to carry him most of the way there.

Rudy has stepped into a river and is being transported. His blood and sweat do not drip down to the road. They fall to backs of the ants who prevent these drops from being a trail. When the ants dissipate in four directions, in eight directions, in sixteen directions, the clues will turn into background noise.

He hears the flapping of wings near his ears. Black shapes. Are they bats? No, not bats at midday. Something else. Something attentive.

He is funneled by 60,000 couriers down Anderson Street, a right turn off the main road. The stevedores carry him a block and then a second.

Even before he grabs the doorknob of the two-story house, he knows the door is unlocked. Even before he steps inside, he knows the place is empty and abandoned.

He can feel the ground again as he ceases to float, ceases to hover. The ants leave him on the porch.

There will be hot water. There will be gauze and band aids. There will be clothes that fit or close enough. He will have nothing of his own to put in his new pants pockets. Nothing to prove his identity.

There will be something to eat. A can that needs a can opener that needs a saucepan that needs a gas flame.

The ants do not follow him inside. Their delivery is complete and now they move on to obfuscate his path.

Rudy wants to sleep, to concede, to allow his eyes to fall shut, but he does not.

He notices the brightness of the peripheries as if a dimmer switch has been turned up and up. They have followed him from the church courtyard along Sixth Avenue and into this house where they are allowed entry.

There are new faces too. Four that sit together where there are no chairs. They are positioned as if around a table. They are holding hands as if at a séance. As Rudy walks through them, he realizes they are saying grace.

26 – Backyard Night Elephant

The backyard night elephant does not want

to hear me sing my solemns

and sing my bleeds

not to spit my psalms through my chipped teeth

the elephant is just a string of lights

haphazardly wrapped around a Ceanothus bush

which is long dead

this string is

attached to a solar charger

when you get up close

you realize

there is nothing there

it is all random

without pattern without shape

but at night

when it glows

it is enough to make the dog piss

on the other side of the lawn.

27 - The Christening of Crows

Rudy takes inventory of the first aid supplies in the house. He finds:

alcohol wipes

tubes of antibiotic cream

rolls of gauze

boxes of Band-Aids, most of which are child sized and in bright colors

tweezers

aspirin

ibuprofen

white tape

first aid scissors with rounded edges and smaller finger holes which he cannot manage

It takes a twenty-minute shower to wash off all the fluids and residue that are on his body. Some of these do not belong to him. The hot water highlights every wound. He feels as if he is rinsing in pickle juice.

He scrapes off caked blood so he can clean the cuts and open areas. He maps all the new bruises which have selected colors independent of their compatriots.

He uses the tweezers to pull out splinters that have dug deep into the fleshy part below his thumb and at various places in his right palm.

He picks out bits of glass and pebbles from the soles of his feet. He is surprised by the number of items he has to dislodge. His feet are left raw and pink. He coats the bottoms with antibiotic cream and wraps them in gauze three layers thick. His feet look like they have come from surgery or from the burn ward.

His torso is adorned with little squares of gauze taped directly to his skin. Like postage stamps have been applied randomly to his body.

Rudy uses all of the alcohol wipes. The evaporating volatiles from the wipes and the antibiotic cream create an invisible chemical current through the house. He has to open the windows in a few of the rooms to bring in fresh air.

He collects all of the clothes that belong to the father of the house. He lays them on the queen bed in the master bedroom upstairs. He sorts them into three piles. One is for items he just cannot use. The second pile is for items he could comfortably wear only around the house to stay warm. The third contains items that he could wear outside without drawing unnecessary attention, without looking like a thief. The man was shaped differently than Rudy. Shorter, thicker around the middle. Shirts and pants have memories that long ago crystallized their shapes and dimensions.

Rudy is grateful the shoes are near his size. But he is several days away from being able to put shoes on his swollen feet.

Rudy walks through the house looking like an entire paint store. If the walls were colorful instead of bland, off-white, some part of him, some extremity, some small patch of skin on a leg or an arm would match the color of that wall. He is an incomplete aggregate chameleon.

Rudy performs a similar inventory on the food supplies. Most of the food in the fridge is questionable. Expired dates on milk and butter and juices and lunchmeat. The pantry is full of cans: vegetables, fruits in syrup, various soups, pastas in bland sauces, chili, beef stew, refried beans.

He pushes the safe-to-eat items into little clusters on the counter, organized primarily by food groups. He considers combinations that could be meals. He makes mental estimates of how many days this will feed him.

The small freezer above the refrigerator holds ice cream and boxes of frozen waffles and some family-sized boxes of frozen lasagna that require an hour to cook. Using the toaster and a sticky bottle of maple syrup from the pantry, he consumes the full box of waffles in one sitting.

The tall freezer in the garage is half full of packages of meat: chicken, steak, pork chops, also fish sticks.

Rudy surveys the backyard from the back steps. Identifying sight lines where neighbors can view any activity in the yard. The left side of the yard, which he believes is the south side, is sheltered from voyeurs.

The peripheries have settled into the house as well. They stagger through the rooms.

Rudy yells at one of them, "You did nothing. You just let it happen."

The periphery puts its hands up to its face covering eyes and cheeks. It ripples as Rudy steps through its image.

After sundown he moves a lawn chair and a cast-iron table into that blind spot. Some of the peripheries wander around the backyard. They look like they are playing croquet but without any mallets or balls.

Rudy has noticed the crows in the neighborhood working as trios. Two on the ground scavenging while a third acts as a spotter or lookout from a high tree perch or a rooftop. The crows in each trio rotate through the day so everyone can eat.

On the third day, sitting in that spot, he has a staring contest with a crow perched on the fence. He recognizes this is a baby crow. Inconsistently colored with fluffed up plumage.

He expects it to holler at Rudy or fly away, but it sits still and silent. A drunken misfit, stuck in its location and its condition.

A second crow, roughly the same height, but sleeker, joins the first. This one flits around the first, initiating transfer of something from its mouth to the younger one. Rudy assumes this is the mother. She prattles and corrects. She repositions herself to keep Rudy in her view.

The mother flies off multiple times, returning with more mouthfuls of nourishment to force down her child's throat. She glides gracefully to the fence each time in showoff arcs. Though she extends her wings to decelerate, her claws hitting the fence are audible. She is a ballet dancer with the orchestra silent and shut down. You can hear all the landings.

In crow terms, Rudy thinks she might be an example of beauty and grace. Taking attentive care of her offspring who looks like some gothic monster or a first-draft gargoyle.

Rudy speaks to them with no expectations of being understood. He names them Grendel and Grendel's Mother. He still does not know what Grendel sounds like on the fifth day at that house.

He is outside early in the morning at the table. His breakfast is some strips of chicken he has marinated in barbecue sauce. He has cooked too much and expects to have leftovers for tomorrow. His wrapped feet are off the ground, supporting no weight. Tomorrow he might try squeezing them into shoes.

A different crow has joined him, watching him from the center of the lawn. This one has moved in a roundabout path to approach him. The crow stops ten feet away.

While its body is still, its dark head adjusts and turns on a steady beat. Rudy finds himself tapping the rhythm with the finger of his left hand on the table top.

He throws a piece of chicken near the crow which flies away into a nearby maple tree. A minute later, the crow returns to the previous spot, inspecting the chicken before devouring it.

The new crow moves closer, six feet away now. It does not fly away after subsequent tosses of food.

Rudy notices an exception to its dark color. An ivory diagonal strip crosses the left side of his head. The crow looks as if it has been marked by a house painter. Perhaps it is the outward aspect of a lost battle.

Rudy thinks of David Bowie's face on the cover of the *Aladdin Sane* album. This crow will never be mistaken for a different crow. He names this brave one Bowie.

Rudy wants to put together a go bag. He knows that he cannot stay here forever and may need to leave suddenly if the previous owners return or nosy neighbors call the police on him. He needs a bag of toiletries, first aid items, small meals that do not need refrigeration or cooking. A survival kit.

He struggles to find the type of bag he is looking for. Even digging through the garage shelves, he locates only briefcases, suitcases, and over the shoulder purses which will not work.

He settles on a backpack which he finds in a small upstairs bedroom. Based on the ribbons and stickers and colorful patterns, he assumes the owner is a young girl. Based on its size and surprising weight, he leans towards early teenage years. The backpack is a light purple with teal accents.

Rudy attempts to dampen the brightness of the backpack by cutting off all the ribbons and removing the small furry creatures attached to the zippers. But the stickers refuse to be removed. He empties the contents on the bed in that same room. Impossibly the contents cover and spill over the bed. There are colored pens, perfume samples, fashion magazines, small figures of animals you might find in a zoo and others that are fictional which he cannot identify. There are hair ties by the dozen along with a hairbrush holding a skein of long black hair. Necklaces and trinket rings. A drawing pad full of sketches of classmates and manga cartoon characters. Folded up notes that he chooses not to read.

He concludes this bag is only safe for nighttime journeys. Even then, it may need to be covered in a dark cloth, a magician's cape for eliminating suspicion.

On the eighth day, Rudy finds a small cache of paper money and quarters in a nightstand drawer in the master bedroom. Roughly $32.

Rudy makes a list of necessary items. He prioritizes

his meager funds. He wants some milk and some cheese and some eggs and more toothpaste.

When he leaves the house for the first time, he has no key, so he does not lock the door. He stands on the porch in the shadows for an hour, hoping to time his emergence unseen. He walks with some false confidence down the walkway and out into the suburban street. He strides under old trees, which connect above to form a network. Branches holding branches above him.

Rudy hears the bold meow of a cat. The call repeats and follows him for several houses. When he looks upward, he is surprised to see a crow eying him. Evaluating him. He thinks the sound may be unrelated until the crow meows at him in perfect feline mimicry. The crow sounds like a good sized cat, enough to scare away other birds. The two of them stay there watching each other for a few minutes. Surveying each other.

The first cat that comes to mind is Garfield, the orange tabby from the cartoons. That is now this crow's name.

Rudy then continues down the street. He hopes to find a grocery store or a drugstore, but settles for a convenience store.

He collects his purchases in a handheld basket. He does his best to estimate the sum and compare this to his budget. His math skills are fuzzy today. The man at the register is patient at updating him with the remaining balance.

"You have $5.29 left."

After three more revised totals, he still has three cents left. Rudy puts the three pennies in his pocket where they are the only residents.

"For luck," he says to the cashier who does not acknowledge this.

Rudy returns to the house along the same route he came. He hears the disturbances in the trees above him again and a few familiar meows. He opens up his grocery bag and removes a package of beef jerky. He tears a piece for himself and then a smaller piece. He looks upward to locate Garfield. Instead, he finds two crows there. They are slightly different in size. The smaller newcomer is a little further away from Rudy.

Then both the crows meow. He cannot tell the two sounds apart.

"So, you have a friend. Maybe a girlfriend."

Rudy tears a second piece so that both crows can eat. He remembers in the cartoons that Garfield had a girlfriend named Arlene so that becomes her name.

He tosses the two pieces of beef jerky onto the sidewalk. The two crows descend without pause and each take their piece. The three of them make their way back to the house, sharing equally the contents of the package which is empty by the time Rudy steps on the front porch.

In the backyard. Rudy hears some squawking and sees two crows splashing in the overnight rainwater collected in a birdbath. This large bowl rests on a raised ceramic column on the right side of the yard, in full view of the second-floor windows of two of the adjacent houses.

Rudy approaches, not wanting to scare off the birds. He identifies the two as Grendel's Mother and Bowie. The two crows are in each other's space. They take turns preening each other's feathers.

Rudy spots Grendel on a fence watching the other two but not joining in. Rudy guesses the trio is a family unit. Later he watches Bowie bring mouthful meals to Grendel.

Rudy gets into a routine of sunrise walks in the neighborhood. He travels in increasingly larger radius loops. Most mornings, he has the streets to himself. Above him, an entourage of crows provides air cover. Sometimes three. Sometimes five.

He is spending evenings in the backyard sharing food with the five crows who bring gifts in return. These gifts include bits of seashell, and cheap jewelry. Sometimes old coins, including one that is British which has crossed the ocean and the continent and somehow the last mile has been carried out by a crow to deliver it here.

There are pieces of plastic, small and broken. Of unknown form and fit and origin. They are purposefully molded and shaped, likely mass produced. Rudy has no idea of their purpose.

Rudy witnesses one of the crows, Arlene, dissipate a periphery when she passes through it. The periphery does not return. The crossing of paths does not seem random. This is a purposeful banishment that the crows make into a sport. When all the crows have joined in, Rudy watches their flight paths like an intricate video game projected in the sky. After two days, all of the peripheries have vanished.

On the twelfth day he notices an unfamiliar crow in the street feasting on the remains of a sub sandwich. This crow pulls wrappers and food onto the pavement to sort the edible from the obstacles. This crow looks younger than Bowie or Garfield, but not with the awkwardness of the baby crow. When it notices the other crows in the sky and treetops above, the newcomer scrambles to work faster.

Rudy hears the car before he sees it. Going many miles above the speed limit of the surface streets. It threads its way between parked cars without reducing speed. Rudy yells at the new crow, "Fly away."

The five other crows circle above the new crow. Four of them are giving a constant barrage of calls, loud and insistent.

The crow on the ground turns its back to the others. It does not fly but only hops. It shields its food from them. It puts as much of the remaining sandwich into his beak as it can hold.

The grill of the car strikes the crow squarely. The bird bounces onto the sidewalk opposite Rudy. The car does not slow down. The car does not stop or turn around. Potentially unaware that it has struck anything.

Rudy runs to the crow. He picks it up from the ground. There is not much blood, but the feathers and wings are in disarray. The bird is so very still. He feels no movement and no heartbeat. Rudy stares into the bird's eyes and sees no sign of life.

None of the other five crows have landed. They are swirling and circling, chanting and screaming.

Rudy is crying tears down his jaw line that fall into his lap. He knows nothing about birds or how to heal a bird.

This is a small broken thing. One of the wings is untouched, but the other has taken the brunt of the damage. In his hand, the injured wing feels soft and malleable. He feels the bone pointing in the wrong direction. No longer a mirror image of the other. The bone is in his grasp, and it loosens and moves in a different direction. He allows it to flow that way in an unobstructed slide until he feels it catch into a natural slot and snap into place.

Rudy's left arm spasms as a bolt of electricity travels through his muscle and his flesh. A few seconds later, a second burst, and then a third of diminishing intensity. There is no fourth burst. The phantom battery is finally depleted.

The crow in his hand wriggles out of his grasp and launches itself up. It lands on top of the street sign. It's claws scrape metal and a high-pitched ping echoes across the empty street.

Rudy makes eye contact with the injured crow. Its silhouette is a mistake. The left wing has been assembled incorrectly, pointing the wrong way. Rudy does not know if this crow can ever fly again. It should not be able to fly again.

"You should be dead," he tells the crow. It rises up again in the sky, making a wide long loop before landing again on the same street sign.

He names the sixth crow Lazarus.

Garfield and Darlene land near Rudy. They bow to him repeatedly while singing a non-feline song. They are not begging for food. Rudy bows back to them.

28 - Your Father Lives in the Mirror Now

In a poorly lit restaurant bathroom in San Antonio, I looked in the mirror and I saw my father.

I saw a receding hairline that was not mine. I saw the smirk that proxies for a smile. I saw wrinkles and frown lines. Our faces were two maps, the same place drawn years apart by different hands.

I had been walking in the heat all day. My shirt was carrying what felt like several pounds of water weight. Like my own camel, a canteen made of cloth. In the mirror, his shirt was similar in style but had a different pattern.

My father reached his hand out toward me, and I swatted it away.

Then I got out of that bathroom. I had not been drinking, but I sure as hell started then. My companions had ordered a round of pints while I was away from the table. I traded my pint for a shot of something stronger. I needed it.

My father ten years gone and this ten years had not been kind to him.

I tell you now, but I did not tell them then. I did not tell them anything. I know this was no dream. No hallucination. This was no allegory and certainly not a Christian allegory like some people try to make everything.

I know where he lives now. I was just too close to the river. Things come up from the river. From flowing waters.

So I moved west and north and ended up here in Tacoma. Telling stories outside of a restaurant. Sitting outside because of new rules and new laws.

No mirrors for me. I piss in the alley instead.

No mirrors in my place either. I brought a woman home once. You seem skeptical. She went into the bathroom to freshen up. She came out quick with a very serious look on her face. She walked through every foot of my place inspecting the walls. She circled back around to me, and she took out one of those little round compact mirrors from out of her purse. She popped it open and held it up to my face.

When she saw my reflection, her soft side returned. She said, "We're all good."

I did not tell her the story about the mirror. That's a surefire way to chase a lady out of your bedroom.

Even so she insisted that all our future dates start during sunlight. I had to get off work early.

She had big old crosses hanging around her neck bouncing on her chest. Banging against my chest, banging against my forehead.

I don't know what I saw in the mirror that day.

I don't think it was really him. I think it was a fraud, an impersonator. Something that traveled by water. Something that picked up a convenient shell. Something lonely.

Damn summer nights here are just perfect. They just go on and on and on. Northern latitudes.

But you do need fireflies. Maybe we could smuggle some in.

29 - Squatter

Rudy falls into a pattern of staying in abandoned houses. He is drawn to empty and unlocked residences. Some sort of built-in radar or infrared night vision goggles. The following of ley lines.

He assumes the places are unlocked before he arrives, and that mechanisms are not undone and freed by his proximity.

Rudy makes a thorough inventory of each home. Is the water running? Has the power been cut? He looks for functioning washers and dryers.

Then on to food. What is still safe to eat and how long will it last.

During the day, he primarily stays inside the house. He avoids awkward conversations with curious neighbors. He clears packages and business flyers off the front porch but does no yardwork.

In one house, he finds an insistent cat shepherding him into the kitchen toward the pantry.

He opens three cans of cat food to make up for missed few meals.

In bathrooms, Rudy looks for toothpaste and soap and razors, and Band-Aids and over-the-counter medications.

He tries to salvage clothing from closets. Clean shirts, and pants, especially underwear and socks. Sometimes the previous residents are shaped too differently to make this work.

He does not turn on televisions or radios or computers. He reads all the magazines he can find. All the comic books. He fights through novels. He keeps a bag packed and ready to go near him.

In a predictable way, the food will run low. In a more random way, the lights will go off as some utility company loses patience with a belated billpayer.

He moves on and moves through neighborhoods. From the Hilltop area down to Proctor with older houses containing terrifying staircases built for tiny feet. Into the newer suburbs in University Place.

He finds the empty places. He finds the ones that let him in.

He shares some of this food with the six crows though he knows they can forage well enough without him. They act as an alarm system. They rotate as sentries on backyard fences or high in the trees or on the rain gutters of the roof.

Rudy is unsure if the peripheries are truly gone, banished to some other world.

He searches each home for money. Cookie jars, the cracks in the sofa, all possible drawers, boxes on top shelves of closets, under mattresses, piggy banks. He has entered this house with no cash or credit cards or even a way to confirm his identity.

When he does find any cash, he spends it that day. Like it was fool's gold. As if it might fail on close scrutiny. Like ice melting in his hands. Like the sense of money and the value of the specific money is soon to expire.

In another house, he finds a closet stacked to the ceiling with jigsaw puzzles. They keep him busy. But he cannot bear to take them apart. It feels like taking the life away from some creature to put it back in its box.

Soon there are not enough tables or countertops. He does puzzles on hardwood floors and on the linoleum until they are also covered entirely. He steps over them carefully, avoiding damage to these colony creatures. When there are no more surfaces, when navigating through the hallways becomes impossible, he moves on to find another house.

When searching for the next place to stay, Rudy walks in deliberate big strides. This part of the city has uneven sidewalks. You must watch where you place your feet or you will crash. Like crossing a complicated Zen garden with inconsistently spaced stones.

The roots of old oak trees have cracked through and erupted through the pavement. They have broken through the restraints and want to walk.

Trees are slow animals. Rocks are slow trees. Everything moves. Everything travels and everything changes.

In some of the parks, the Canada geese have claimed territory. They are plumped from the discarded food of picnickers. They are descendants of dinosaurs. They are dinosaurs.

They chase children. They drive large dogs off the grassy areas. Six crows in the sky warn Rudy when he approaches an especially surly pair of dinosaurs. Their redirections are clear.

The streets in this part of Tacoma are especially narrow. Approaching cars manage a silent ballet, a polite pantomime to let one pass. Some of the vehicles have been parked here so long that Rudy can see extensive spiderwebs from the wheel wells down to the curb. Children's toys are lost there. Perhaps other treasures, but no one is putting their hand through there.

When Rudy approaches a person walking in the opposite direction, that person crosses the street to avoid him without speaking a word. They do not make eye contact.

He finds a clean side mirror of a car and turns it to view himself. While there is some distortion, he does not think he looks dangerous or menacing.

Today, this avoidance happens too many times. He alters his route to walk down an alley instead. He is closer to kitchens and back doors. He hears pots and pans in random percussion. He hears laughing and sometimes yelling.

Small shadows move on the ground around him. Six little eclipses.

Most days he speaks to no one. He worries that he is forgetting how.

Is he losing his language?

Near a back porch, he finds a kiwi tree. He pulls three leather-coated fruits from a reachable branch and puts them in his pack. He does not know how to identify those that are ripe.

He is watched and stalked by cats. He is barked at by dogs. His brain points him south today.

In the backyard of yet another house, he sits cross-legged in the wet grass. The lawn is losing a battle to clover and buttercups. There is a fountain in the center plaza, but the pump needs replacing. Rudy does not want to spend his scarce funds on a pump.

Military transport planes from Joint Base Lewis-McChord pass overhead. This location is under the elbow of their flight path. He watches a C-17 plane bank and turn more than 90 degrees, roaring the entire time.

The crows do not like these moments and hide somewhere low to the ground.

His mind imagines that this plane turns because someone has spotted him and has him in their sights. But no bombs are dropped, and no shots are fired.

This is a path of a river in the air traveled by a series of high-flying steamboats. The house rumbles. He would not be surprised to see a roof shingle tossed into the yard.

Everything rattles in time with the planes until the planes are gone. Then it is just clover and buttercups and less anxious crows.

It is sunlight until it is rain. It is day until it is night.

30 - The Year that Everyone Who Died Had to Die Twice

There is a boundary between this world and the next one. When the amount of passage gets too heavy, the boundary between the worlds gets thin.

Too thin.

There are places where the old rules do not stay enforced. This can happen during a war. During a pogrom.

During a plague.

The physicists have a term for this.

Quantum tunneling. A small but non-zero probability that an object can be found on the wrong side of the wall.

As if it had passed through the barrier like a ghost.

On a Sunday, we heard the announcement that the actress Tanya Roberts had died. She was remembered for television shows like *Charlie's Angels* and *That 70s Show*. Movies like *The Beastmaster* and *Sheena of the Jungle*.

Not an actress of tremendous skill, but one of distracting beauty. Men who remember their younger versions being enamored of her younger version toast in her honor.

A 65-year-old goddess was taken at a time when so many have been taken.

On Monday, Tanya Roberts' publicist announces that there has been a mistake. She is still alive. He corrects this on the news broadcasts and online.

Then late Monday evening, we hear a new announcement that Tanya Roberts has died. Her second chance lasted a mere day. A brief resurrection.

It is a terrible thing to be mourned and then resurrected and then mourned once again with some tentative grieving in case the toggling continues. I could cry for you once but twice is too much to ask.

Obituaries will be written in sand. The second date is crossed out and replaced. This is the year where everyone who died had to die twice. Not zombies. Not vampires. Just honest mistakes. We should have waited longer to fill out the form. To mark the time from the clock.

This year will take forever. There will not be enough time, not enough days of the week if everyone must die twice. We bury them with garlic and holy water. But also, with a panic button. There is a switchboard and there is a monitoring station. Dig up that man for this is only his first death. A false tease. A foreshadowing. He has a little more time left. The next of kin got a practice run. Have they already divided up his belongings, his minor fortune.

No one gets a panic button on the inside of the coffin for the second funeral. Should we burn the bodies? These are plague year rules. The city frowns on this. The cemeteries have waiting lists. And repeat customers. The graveyards are hiring and function like clockwork. A man who can handle a shovel is a man who can feed his family.

We realize later that we have overreacted. It was only that one woman. We will not bring this up with each other again. This was not the year where everyone who died had to die twice. This was the month we were idiots.

31 – Intruder Alert

At roughly 10 AM on a… who knows what day of the week. Those seven different words are meaningless to many now and especially to Rudy.

He hears a chorus of six crows, actually five because Grendel is still silent, making a very similar sound. A screech meant to be heard and repeated. An alarm.

He can distinguish their individual voices. They sing together but they do not harmonize. They have never made this kind of noise.

Rudy looks out the front room window. Parked in the driveway is a four-door sedan that he had not heard approach.

A man in a light blue dress shirt and tan khakis gets out of the car. He opens the backseat door behind the driver's side and retrieves a clipboard.

The crows continue with their alarm. Three of them are on the rain gutter above Rudy's head. He can hear their talons scraping on the gutters' metal edge.

The other three are in the air. Low altitude satellites swooping in tight circles.

The man in the blue shirt stops and scans the sky. The crows have his attention.

Rudy runs to the kitchen counter and grabs his go bag. He bursts out the door to the backyard and toward the side of the fence that borders the street.

The bag goes over the fence first. Rudy follows. He does not land like a superhero or a gymnast or like an elegant bird. He lands like something tossed without aiming. All shoulders and knees into a mass of blackberry bushes. Minor scratches but nothing injured.

With the bag in hand, he points away from the house that he has now abandoned. His stride is too long, so his posture is poor.

A block away, he has collected an entourage. Two then four then finally six black shapes around him. A rotating shield. Six electrons in a nucleus. Carbon.

Rudy regrets the loss of the home. He had two, maybe three months of food reserves in the cupboard and freezer. He was only halfway through the tall bookshelf of romance novels. He thinks he could adequately write one himself. Now that he knows the shape of those novels.

The crows have calmed down and become quiet. He only hears them only as breezes and currents close to his face. They are going where he goes. He looks for a place to collect himself and calm his breathing. A park or a bus shelter or some green space.

32 – Any Ocean Will Do

I wait in line outside. No customers are allowed inside the restaurant these days.

There are several feet between each person in line. The customer at the front is having a hard time being heard over the sounds of cars rushing past. We are all in masks. It is raining because it is always raining.

When I have ordered, I wait on the side again. Well-spaced from the other customers.

We all regard each other with caution and distrust. We are all suspects, potential murderers. We have taken some risk to even be here. Will you be the reason I get sick? Will you be the reason I die or someone in my family dies? We didn't use to think of each other like that.

When my number is called, I collect a plastic bag full of smaller plastic containers. The person at the counter and I are careful not to touch hands. We don't even make eye contact.

You are driving because you know these streets. The layout of the city. My navigation skills are terrible, and I can get lost so easily. I also panic when driving down the very narrow residential streets with parked cars crushing from both sides.

My claustrophobia still kicks in when you are driving. I can just close my eyes.

We find a place to park. This is no lovers' lane. This is midday so we are not pointed at the sunrise or the sunset. We are pointed west to the Pacific, which we cannot see from here, but any ocean will do.

We park out in the open so no one can sneak up on us. Post-apocalyptic rules.

I rinse my hands with hand sanitizer. The scent fills the car and leaves traces on my hands. It becomes another ingredient in our picnic lunch, a condiment. It is a bit of garnish. It is a bit of garlic. It is a bit of onion. It is cilantro and parsley, and it is soy sauce.

We lay towels across our laps. We have chosen sloppy food. We will have to do laundry after we eat.

There are multiple courses, multiple sauces and things to cut. We have brought real silverware.

There are not enough flat surfaces in the car. This seems an intentional design decision. We balance items on the dashboard. We tuck things into the pockets of the door.

We feel safe here, when the doors are locked, and the windows are rolled up. Safe in our submarine. Our personal atmosphere is sealed from the outside world. We can observe and glance around while we eat. This is the ocean floor we are resting on. There is fauna and flora to identify. I can recite genus and species.

There are other submarines. Maybe they are having a picnic too. They do not engage with us and do not approach us. You never know who is infected. Who is vaccinated. Who is taking risks. Again, post-apocalyptic rules.

I tell you about the submarine. You think we are in a spacecraft. The air outside is unreliable and deadly. We stare out portholes at an alien landscape full of unfamiliar creatures. We get to come up with the genus and species names instead of remembering them. We are scientists and explorers. We have no return ticket.

The air inside our vehicle is our greatest asset, but it is not infinite. No one but the two of us have been in this car for a year. I miss going into pubs and restaurants and movie theaters. Anywhere really. I just need different ceilings and different skies.

When we get home. I will call my brother. A video call. We are each in our own bunker miles and miles away, trying to outlast the bombs.

I don't recognize him anymore. These years have aged us prematurely. They are dog years. Each one counts as seven.

There has been a fracture in the world. The time before and the time after have different architects and different measurements.

The picnic was a good idea. We talk about where to go next week. A change in restaurant and a change in where to park. We talk like small-time criminals trying to avoid routine so we don't get caught.

We may choose to point east next time, toward the Atlantic, though you cannot see it from here. Any ocean will do.

33 - Upside Down on Hooks

Rudy finds a one-story house with a car crashed into the front.

The old green Pontiac two-door has left a hole in the house large enough for a person to climb through. The driver's side door is open, and the keys are still in the ignition.

This is a solid metallic machine. You can sit on the hood or the roof on a summer night watching meteor showers without leaving a dent. The kind of vehicle that is surface of the sun hot to the touch during summer days. The windows roll up manually. There are multiple ashtrays, one for each passenger.

The passenger side headlight is embedded in the wall of the house. The damage to the side of the Pontiac is obstructing that wheel from turning. Structural damage. The wall of the house has taken a direct hit through wooden siding, drywall, and even a thin layer of sunflower wallpaper. A door has been made. The hole is oval and uneven.

The entryway is the mouth of a cave. The cross-section of a tunnel made by a prehistoric, fast-moving serpent. The entry point or exit point of a missile.

Rudy's intuition tells him not to enter the place. That this is not a potential residence. Not a safe place.

Rudy enters through the hole.

The lights are still on inside, but all the windows are boarded up with sheets of plywood. The front door is barricaded by an unplugged refrigerator. The freezer half has defrosted, leaving a large puddle of gray water.

He finds muddy footprints leading from the entry point into the house. These are actual barefoot footprints. He kneels down and determines they are a long dried. The tracks go all through the house with more mud than a pair of feet could seemingly hold. He finds a few wet leaves alongside the prints.

Every point of entry to the house except for the hole is blocked by nailed boards or furniture. He finds a master bedroom and two small rooms full of tiny furniture with toys on the floor.

In a bathroom, he sees large handwriting in red on the mirror.

"No one comes in no one goes out."

At first, he thinks it might be written in blood, but he finds the writing instrument on the counter. A tube of bright red lipstick.

He clears the obstacles to the door leading to the garage. Inside are two immaculate cars, one of which is a station wagon.

Four bicycles hang upside down on hooks. Two of them are too small for an adult. Bells on the front and empty baskets on the back.

Rudy finds very little to replenish his backpack in the master bedroom. He takes a tube of toothpaste and a few disposable razors. Based on color and packaging, the razors were intended for female legs and not male faces.

He takes one of the bicycles too.

A strange logic tells him to exit the way he entered. To leave by the garage door would not set things back to zero. He struggles to fit the bicycle through the impact point.

The torn sunflower wallpaper offers resistance as he passes. It feels like leaves and branches preventing his departure.

Rudy finds the appropriate angle to navigate the handlebars and wheels through the hole in the wall.

He is surprised to find the sun has gone down. He heads west, peddling up the hills and coasting back down.

34 - One of Many Rainsongs

To talk about the rain in Tacoma is to not talk about it enough. It is not that it is always raining but that it is always threatening to rain.

Everything is muted and gray as a result. The rain seems to suspend in the air like a curtain of beads. The rain does not fall on you. You walk through the rain.

Your beauty is covered in jackets and hoodies. To see your decorative flamboyance, I need to be in the same room as you. When we take off our outer layers and they're hanging and dripping over the backs of chairs.

Perhaps it's just the two of us in the room. Wet clothes on the floor. The rain is like delicate mice feet on the roof and on the windows.

It is typically not a hard rain in the Pacific Northwest.

Rain here is rarely a violence.

With the masks that people wear today, there is even less of you to see. The town is made anonymous with the social distancing.

You seem further away, an imprecise image through my rain-streaked glasses.

When crows reach maturity, their feathers become waterproof. The drops won't pierce their armor. I envy them.

To walk slowly in the rain with no umbrella is an act of defiance. Snow will absorb sounds and make the world quieter. The rain just talks over the soundtrack of the world. It asserts audio dominance.

When someone from Tacoma tells you a story, they won't tell you if it was raining. You should assume it was unless they have specifically said otherwise.

I will walk you home in the rain. I did not even need to say it was raining. We will take our time.

We will talk standing on the front steps of your apartment building. It will smell like cigarette smoke and pot smoke and dog piss because those purse dogs are not waterproof and reluctant to brave the wet night.

I will walk back to my place alone again. I will walk slowly. I won't let the rain win.

35 – Time Tricks

Rudy is riding the bicycle through Old Town, admiring the spacious houses with green lawns. Some qualify as mansions. He can see Commencement Bay off to his right and a set of freight train tracks in between.

He has used his newfound transportation to put a few miles between himself and the house with a hole in the wall. He is scouting. He is coasting.

A large pickup truck pulls out from a driveway and strikes the front wheel of his bicycle. Rudy tumbles over the hood of the truck. He bends his knees and elbows and tucks his head. He folds up like an armadillo and rolls to a stop.

The bicycle flies forward and collides with a parked car. The front wheel of the bicycle comes off, and the rim is bent.

The driver of the truck stops his vehicle and rushes out to Rudy. He is a large man wearing mostly denim with work boots.

"Are you okay? I never saw you. And you with no helmet. I'm so sorry."

Rudy unveils his face from the protective ball. He has never seen this man before.

The driver stands back up and says, "Is that you Rudy? I guess I owe you two apologies now."

Rudy does not smile and does not frown. "How do you know who I am?"

"Of course you wouldn't know. You haven't met me yet. But I've met you. It's hard to explain and we have some time for that."

He pulls Rudy up to his feet far too easily.

"First we have to get you out of the road and see how your bike faired."

They inspect the bike, which looks like it was hit by a train and not a truck. It looks like evidence of disaster. It looks like salvage.

The man says, "I think your bike is fucked. No one's ever gonna ride it again. How long have you had it?"

"Not long. Not my bike."

The man looks closely at Rudy.

"I didn't steal it from anyone. I found it in an abandoned house in the garage."

"Is that where you're living?"

"No. No one is living there, and no one should live there. Something happened. something wrong. Someone had broken into the house using a car. I didn't feel safe there."

"Well, you can stay with me. I owe you that, old friend."

He walks Rudy back to the truck. "My name is Harvey Burgess. My life is complicated. I think yours is too."

143

Harvey continues, "Seeing what happened to that bicycle, I don't know how you just got up with nothing broken. You don't feel anything broken do you?"

"No. Just a few scratches on my knees. A little blood. Mostly my pants took the brunt of it."

"I guess I owe you a pair of pants too."

Harvey talks as he drives, "This is the first time you've met me, but not the first time I've met you. You don't understand. I don't live events in the right sequence. It is not a linear path, but the overall direction for me is backward. I am so often missing the context of the day. I have to wing it. If a girl kisses me, I do not push her away. She is probably my girlfriend, but I don't have the right history. It will all make sense eventually. I tell you this, so you don't think I'm crazy or drunk when I look confused."

Harvey drives with the windows rolled down. "This drive through the city is more interesting, more surreal if you pretend there's only one bus and somehow it keeps getting in front of you. To boast about its ability to navigate more swiftly than you. To block your way for a short while. Here he is in front of us now. You would think something so big and unwieldy would not be so sneaky. That bus driver has maps that I do not have. He is keeping us from beer and desserts."

"What kind of desserts?" Rudy asks.

"On a warm day like this with no air conditioning in the car, we will get some soft serve ice cream. Today ice cream is compulsory. No substitutions will be accepted."

"And there he is again. Somehow, he has outflanked us to swing his ass across two lanes and impede our journey. There must be streets only open to him. Ones that look like walls and dead ends to amateur drivers like me. Well done, mister bus driver. I will temporarily pass you on the left while you plan once more to cheat time and space to arrive early where I am going even when I do not know where I am going."

"Hey Rudy, did you get a look at the bus driver? He has a head like an old pug. I don't mean like a pug's head. I mean the entire dog minus the legs. He is gray and lumpy and asymmetric."

Harvey has a business. It is written on the side of his truck: *Harvey Burgess – Factotum.*

He lets Rudy sleep on the couch, but Rudy does not sleep.

Together they transport boxes. They load and unload for people who pay cash. Harvey presses a few twenty-dollar bills into Rudy's hands.

"Don't spend this now. Save it for when you need food."

They carry stacks of wood to someone who is building a fence. They transport ten crates of noisy chickens and leave them in someone's backyard. The owner is in the kitchen of his house and does not come out to inspect the delivery until Harvey and Rudy have closed the gate behind them. When they reach the truck, there is an envelope of green bills resting on the driver's seat.

In the evening after dinner, Rudy is outside, throwing scraps of food to the six crows who have encircled him.

Harvey steps out on the back patio and all six crows launch up into the trees. He says, "Whoa. I know them."

The crows are hollering, squawking, and barking at Harvey.

"It seems they know me too, which should not be possible." He walks under a tree where Bowie is batting his wings before leaping up into higher level of the tree.

"Which way do your clocks spin little ones?" Harvey asks.

Then Grendel's Mother is in the same tree but low and close. Harvey is reminded of a different day. He backs away from the tree.

He addresses Rudy. "If I give them some food, maybe they will tolerate me but for today, I will leave you and them alone."

Harvey puts a stack of books on the table next to the couch. There is a deck of playing cards which Rudy picks up using a napkin to avoid direct contact. He finds a junk drawer in the kitchen and hides the cards there.

The truck bed is empty and Harvey is talking again. "Listen, my friend. Once when I was younger, I found myself employed by... well it does not matter. I did not ask too many questions. I was on the back of a jeep in a small town in Kenya, Africa. While we drove through town, my eyes darted around with so much to see, and I was being paid to see things before they happen so I can make sure they did not happen. There was a beautiful Black woman in a bowler hat and a sharp suit in the middle of the road directing traffic. She was a cop, and she carried a large gun."

"For a moment, I thought my heart was stolen, but she was the undercard. Just the appetizer. Because then I saw the young woman with the machete. Her hair was cut short, and her skirt was more of a sash.

She was all legs. I did not know they could be that long. She carried the machete as an offensive weapon in her left hand. Nothing and no one would be hunting her. There were men, mere shadows compared to her, following a safe distance behind. They were like hyenas or vultures, trying to curry her favor, her attention, a portion of her spoils. None of them would have been a match for me. I very nearly jumped off the back of that jeep and followed her down that road. I would've been willing to invest days or months or even years to earn her trust. For her to put down that machete and hold both my hands in hers. I dreamt a whole life right there. I suspect it would've been a short one. Terrifying and wonderful. Maybe my digestive system would've failed the first time I shared a meal with her family. I think about this every day."

Rudy asks, "Wait, did this thing happen in my future or your future? When were you in Kenya?"

"That is a good question. An exceedingly good question. Really it is not always a direction of time going backward for me. So, it could be either way. I believe I was older than I am now."

Harvey's voice gets louder, "And again that bus has beat us to this place. He goes too slow for this road to rub it in. He is a fantastic tortoise and I am a foolish hare. I think cough cough. I think he has only victories and misses out cough cough on the cough joy of overcoming cough."

Harvey stops talking altogether and pulls the truck over.

In a softer voice, Harvey says, "This just came out of nowhere. Can't catch my breath. Some crud in my lungs cough, cough my throat." He holds his chest and closes his eyes. "Can you drive a stick my friend?"

"Badly, but I can get us back to your place."

"Not there cough cough to the hospital. This is very bad. I cannot breathe right, I feel like I'm drowning."

Rudy stays in second gear most of the way to St. Joe's hospital up on the hill.

Harvey tells Rudy, "Don't come in. This is not a place that is welcoming visitors unless they are sick." His coughing starts up again. "Just take my truck back to my place and wait for me. Well actually I know that you won't. Please leave my truck there. Use the money in your pocket. There's a little more in the glove box, all yours. I have a feeling that I will meet someone who will be able to drive me home. Do not worry, my friend. I do not die today or even soon. I already know the day I die. Anyway, I still need to meet you for the first time in a few months. I will talk to you then. Before you leave, I would like to apologize. I did not know then. You do not sleep and you are chased, and you are accompanied. Again, I'm sorry in advance for what I will do."

In the glove box, Rudy finds the stack of 20s which he put in his pants pockets. He tries to stay at Harvey's place, to prove his prediction wrong, but he is restless. He leaves the truck keys on the kitchen counter and walks west toward the setting sun.

36 – The Best Sandwich

Rudy reads the six-item menu of a food truck parked on an empty lot. He is eager to transform the bills in his pocket into a hot meal. A hedonistic choice. Something not frozen or canned.

The food truck is basically a little trailer manned by one person. A woman with a thick Russian accent. Dark hair pulled away from her face.

Rudy orders a cheeseburger and a side of French fries.

After taking his money, she points to a man sitting at one of the benches.

She says, "He waits every day for 45 minutes for the same sandwich that I make."

Rudy asks the man if it is a good sandwich.

The man also has a Russian accent. He has light brown hair and mustache. He is smoking a cigarette while looking off into the distance and not looking at the woman at all.

He says, "The best sandwich."

She makes Rudy's cheeseburger, but she also works on various processes or pieces of the complex sandwich. These steps include grilling onions, toasting the bread on the grill, retrieving a bottle of mayonnaise.

She has almost finished the sandwich when she says, "Oh, I have forgotten the eggs."

She walks out of the trailer and around the corner to a refrigerator unit. She pulls out two brown eggs. She cracks them one handed on the grill. Throws down some oil and begins frying those eggs.

The cheeseburger is done and served. Rudy has time to eat all of the burger plus an unreasonably sized order of French fries while the man continues to wait and smoke in silence. Still looking off in the distance.

Rudy hears sizzling on the grill and the giggle of a busy woman as he walks away.

Rudy has not eaten all his French fries. Many have been stuffed into his pockets. As he walks, he throws them on the pavement ahead of him and behind him. A six-man squadron descends and eats them.

Young Grendel is confused and he picks up what he thinks is a French fry, but it is a discarded cigarette. He swaggers around with it in his mouth, not able to quite chew it or devour it. It looks like he is smoking and it looks like he is talking while he is smoking. He becomes frustrated when he realizes that this is not food.

37 - Nameless

With very little money, Rudy walks into a grocery store. A woman with a mask wearing an apron displaying the store's name and logo steps in front of Rudy. Her name tag says Ginger. She points a handheld device at his forehead and for a second, he braces to be shot.

"Just a second young man." The device beeps twice and the woman reads the little display.

"That's a funny number. Well, at least you don't have a fever." She steps out of his way.

"I hope you find what you're looking for."

A redheaded girl stands behind him in the checkout line at the grocery store. She is a young woman in her early 20's but in his mind, she is the redheaded girl. Rudy has only a few items on the conveyor belt. Only things that do not need heat or refrigeration.

She has packages of pasta, canned red sauce, a loaf of bread, cheese, and some ice cream. She glances over his purchases and figures out what his selections mean. She claims him then and there. She invites him to come home with her.

"I will make spaghetti just don't tell me your name." Her hair is an unnatural red and not straight in any place. An awkward in-between length grown out of a haphazard home haircut. Her smile is crooked, and her dimples are out of alignment. She is short and she walks like she is stomping on ants.

He carries her bag and his bag and follows her. She leads them up a walkway to a single-story house that sprawls in four directions so there is little space between its outer walls and the wooden fence on three sides.

The front door is locked, and she has no key. A tall man in red sweatpants and a Hawaiian shirt answers the door. He has a long but well-maintained goatee.

She smiles up at the man inside who is frowning instead. He hands Rudy a small, unused votive candle.

"What does this smell like?" he asks Rudy.

"What?"

"Just tell me what you smell."

"Grapefruit," Rudy replies.

"Close enough," says the man at the door. "You can come in."

Rudy follows her in and follows her around. He helps unload the bags in the kitchen.

She makes good spaghetti though very under-spiced. He eats two huge platefuls. She is visibly pleased and eats just as much as he does. There are a few other people in the house, but they do not introduce themselves and they do not share the meal.

After the meal, she pulls him into her room. She undresses him then, not in a sexual way or a romantic way. More like a nurse would for someone too injured to remove his own clothes. She does not ask permission.

She carries the clothes down the hall to the laundry room, violating any color or fabric separation rules.

The evening is more innocent than he expects. She plays music by The Cure and some other bands he does not recognize.

She gets up and flips the record. She sits down beside him and presses his right hand against her forehead.

"Feel my forehead."

This is his first real contact with her skin. Her skin is ambient temperature and smooth.

"Is it hot?"

He assures her that it is not which disappoints her greatly. She stomps away killing any indoor insects. She puts on a different record.

The redheaded girl goes to the doctor on a regular basis. She gets tested for diabetes. She gets tested for high blood pressure. She relays her suspicions that she has contracted some tropical disease though she has never left the state of Washington.

Blood draws are a bit of a thrill. She puts on extra makeup and a splash of perfume. She wears clean black tights and chews minty gum on the way to the doctor's office.

She judges the phlebotomist for their skill and care. She winks at them and flirts with them regardless of their gender. She hates to confirm her name at the doctor's office. She is asked to repeat it, to prove it with identification. It seems like someone else's name now.

You are not a hypochondriac if you keep your thoughts to yourself. She only shares her concerns with Rudy, her housemates, and of course various medical professionals. Doctor office co-pays and lab tests are recurring expenses for her like groceries or magazine subscriptions.

She worries daily about running a fever. She asks her friends to feel her forehead. She keeps no thermometer in the house because their numbers betray her. They contradict her.

"Me and the mercury tend to disagree," she tells the doctor.

She tells Rudy about her job. She is often late, and she calls out sick frequently. All day, she dreams of just going home.

When Rudy tries to tell her his name, he gets a face full of fingers. She does find out what he used to be. He presents an inventory of his past occupations and useful skills. In her mind, she calls him the butcher. In his mind, she is still the redheaded girl.

First thing in the morning, the redheaded girl asks him to feel her forehead.

Does she have a fever?

She does not have a fever.

This is the third morning and there has never been a hint of fever. Mostly she does not want to go to work.

She has one of the four bedrooms in the house and has also claimed most of the bathroom counter. The living room splits off in four separate ways, one for each bedroom. They are like four points on a compass, but they are not aligned with true north and not aligned with the four serpentine towers of St. Joe's Hospital. Tacoma is not built on a grid.

The redheaded girl occupies the one that is roughly northeast. She has a responsibility as a guardian of that direction. That means of approach. She is an inheritor, not the first. The one before her, the one she never met, was a nurse.

The nurse had been the first resident of the northeast wing to cede her name and to acknowledge the shortness of times. She had seen too many sheets pulled over faces. She was tired of the dead and dying having names.

None of the people living here have names. They have not shared their names because life is temporary and transitory. It hurts less when people leave or die, if you do not know their names.

On the fourth morning, she trusts him enough to give him money for shopping while she is at work. She is late to work and asks him to get some beer. Something dark enough you can't see through. Later, there are beer bottles on the couch and bottle caps on the floor,

Rudy asks one of her housemates, the man with the goatee, "Am I the first?"

The man responds, " I think you're asking if you are the only one. A typical guy's mistake. Am I special? Was she waiting for me? None of that matters and none of that is real. You have been rescued and that is enough. Many others have not been. Listen. None of us are going to die of old age. All of us have lost someone, probably several someones. And by lost, I don't just mean deceased. I think of friends I have lost contact with and where they are. Are they on different islands or have they been buried."

The man pauses so he can bring his volume back down. "So as long as you are in her good graces, you can stay here. A friend of hers is a friend of ours. And someone that makes her happy will get you kindness beyond mere tolerance."

It is morning again. His arm has fallen asleep under her weight, but the rest of him is jealous of the sleep.

The girl, the young woman, has numbed him, and he does not want to disturb her. When she does wake, she looks him over to make sure he is real, that he is still there.

She says, "I don't feel well. I think I have a fever. Can you feel my forehead?"

He checks and she is of an absolutely normal temperature. When he tells her this, she frowns as she always frowns. The early morning request is a piece of domestic predictability. A substitute for a morning kiss.

"I guess I do have to go to work then." With her long nightgown down past her knees she walks out to the hallway into the bathroom.

Rudy sits up and thinks about how he has not been thinking at all. He has just been staring into a dark room. He tries to massage some feeling back into his right arm. He hears the shower turn on.

Before she leaves for work, she tells him, "I used to work at a bookstore, but then no one was shopping anymore in stores, so I got a job in a government office working with women who have worked in the same space for thirty or more years. They were very glad to have someone new to tell their stories to. They are greedy with my time on my fifteen-minute breaks. I pretended to be a smoker for a week to get outside, but they followed me with umbrellas."

"They're sweet old ladies. Our desks have been pushed into the corners of the office now to maximize separation distance. Like kids that would fight if they were too close. There were six of us but now there are only four. No one talks about the other two anymore. Taboo subjects. I asked them to not call me by my name."

"No, I'm not going to slip up and tell you now. I was not feeling good yesterday in the afternoon and asked one of my coworkers to feel my forehead. She told me that was not funny, and she gave me lots of space after that."

The residents of the house gather in the living room for movie night. Rudy has met two of them already: the girl with the red hair who he is sharing a room with and the large man who opened the door to admit him.

One of the housemates is a woman with short wavy hair, a tank top showing biceps to rival Rudy's, a scar or birthmark on her left arm bisects a bright green, tropical fish tattoo. Rudy can't tell if the tattoo or the mark was there first.

The last member of the group is a middle-aged man wearing a purple robe with a hotel chain logo. Underneath the robe he wears a T-shirt with Harpo Marx grinning with mischief. He has to explain to Rudy who Harpo Marx is.

The other two do not exchange names or make introductions. They stare him down, sizing him up. Rudy asks, "Would it just would be easier if you at least had nicknames."

The middle-aged man says, "I got this."

He sits on a recliner chair. There are two other recliners in the room. The muscular woman sits on the floor. Rudy and the redheaded girl share a loveseat.

"Our names are not important. We are not our names. In fact, we are not the first to hold these places in this house. Four seats. Four bedrooms." He gestures down the four hallways that lead to their four rooms.

"Four corners, four quadrants, four directions of wind, four seasons…"

"Four horsemen," Rudy adds.

The room is quiet. The middle-aged man frowns and then restarts as if Rudy had not spoken. "Four Beatles, four hobbits from the Shire, four heads up on Mount Rushmore, four wheels on a car, four legs on a dinosaur." He points his index finger at Rudy. "You are only here until she tires of you or until you…" He waves his right hand, "screw up."

The man from the front door passes around beer bottles, and large bowls of popcorn. The middle-aged man puts a videotape into the VHS player attached to the television. He conceals the label of the tape and the box that it came from.

As the opening credits roll, the audience realizes the film is *The Masque of the Red Death* from 1964 starring Vincent Price. Loosely based on the Edgar Allan Poe story. The group groans with the realization. The redhead girl says, "This is in bad taste, even for you."

The middle-aged man smirks. This was his anticipated result, a small victory. "When it's your turn, we can again dive into the deep reservoir of Cary Grant films."

The muscular woman says, "Vincent Price over Cary Grant seems a very mustache influenced decision. Maybe Cary will show up at the end of this one and save the day."

The room is very quiet and attentive during the entire film. There are no breaks to get another beer or empty a bladder.

At the end of the film, a line of brightly colored figures marches single file along a desolate landscape. Each figure by its color represents a disease, a plague. The final words from Poe's story on the screen: "And darkness and decay and the Red Death held illimitable dominion over all." The man who selected the film explains this thoroughly to the group.

The housemates scan each other, assessing wardrobe selections.

Next to Rudy on the couch, the redheaded girl asks, "Who played the girl again?"

"Jane Asher," the middle-aged man responds. "She and Paul McCartney were a thing. Almost got married. She caught him cheating one day. She has several Beatles songs written about her."

"Why did he lose interest in her?" Rudy asks.

"This is right after Paul died in a car crash. Or one of the Pauls died. More likely she had been with one of the clones."

"Did you say clones?" the man from the door asks.

"Yes, I did. I've been researching this and I'm halfway through a screenplay on this topic. I call it *The McCartney Clones*."

He waits for a reaction. The redheaded girl laughs first. She shakes the couch and loses her breath. She leans her hard head into Rudy's ribs. Then Rudy laughs too, but he is just laughing at her.

The author of the proposed screenplay continues, "See, they found a Paul McCartney dead on the road. When the Beatles were brought to see the body, to ID the body, there is another Paul McCartney there. A bit sobering to see yourself lying dead on the pavement. I'm very happy with the dialogue in that scene. Paul changes there, he is never the same person. Begins to outwrite John, especially on volume because there are more Pauls. The clones work in shifts. Those later albums have songs where Paul plays all the instruments. It's not overdubbed, there are actually multiple Pauls in the studio playing together. This freaks John out. He first turned to LSD and then a guru and then Yoko and then heroin. The story is as much about John as it is about Paul."

All the listeners are laughing now. Rudy's shirt is striped with mascara from the redheaded girl. This is the best way to remove mascara.

The man from the door says, "There is not enough beer in the world to get me drunk enough to read that, or heaven forbid to watch a movie version."

The woman with the biceps says, "Fortunately next week will be an action movie and it will be much better than this."

38 – The Testimony of Birds

She played a record

of her own voice

in the background.

She overloaded those frequencies

so I could not hear

what she was saying.

Perhaps she was ordering

the movement of troops

or arranging a sly rendezvous

but it all sounded like

the testimony of birds.

39 – Tall Tales

Rudy and the redheaded girl are sitting lazy and slouchy on the couch. Her housemates are in their own rooms. She giggles and tries to sit upright and proper but slides into another sloppy pose.

She starts to tell a story. "You may notice the tattoos on my arms and on my legs. They're a bit faded, and it's not because I went to a cheap place to have them done. It's because they are secondhand tattoos. I got them from an older woman who just got a corporate job and couldn't have them show on her arms and legs. So I got them. These tattoos are therefore older than I am and some of them, I don't even know what they mean. This one here on my upper arm is of a great blue heron. A beautiful bird, but I don't know anything about these birds. I can't explain. I got the tattoos but not the backstories."

She pauses long enough for him to know the story is done. She drinks deep from a beer bottle. Some ends up on her shirt. She stares at him, inviting him to match her tale.

Rudy says, "I just watched your housemate tumble out of a rolling car crash. No other car. She just brushed herself off and walked into the house. She looked beautiful and angry."

The redheaded girl interjects, "Yes, someone is trying to kill her."

Rudy continues, "This is the second time I have seen her do this. The car was mostly gone. The largest piece left was the steering wheel."

Then Rudy drinks and leans back. The redheaded girl shakes her head unimpressed.

She counters with a lower voice, speaking with more pauses between words. "I was living in a house in the Proctor district. No, I was housesitting for a few months while the owner traveled to South America."

"The place had a large basement which included a room with a washer and dryer. One night, I went down the stairs to put my wet clothes in the dryer. Somehow, when I came back up, I went up the wrong stairs. On the ground floor, nothing was familiar. The furniture, the layout of rooms, not the same place at all. All my stuff was gone. I recognized none of it."

"I walked out the front door onto the porch. I did not recognize the basket of hanging flowers. This was a different neighborhood. The houses on either side and the ones across the street were nothing I had seen before. At the corner, I checked the street sign. Both cross streets were just numbered streets, so... this did not help."

"I walked back in the house and went back down to the basement. I searched methodically, but there was only one set of stairs. I pushed on walls and looked behind the hot water heater, but I found no other way out. I closed my eyes for a full minute, two minutes, hoping to reset the world."

"Upstairs it was still that strange foreign home. I went up and down the stairs five… six… maybe a dozen times. Faster and faster. More and more manic. I was sobbing. I had left my cell phone upstairs in the place I knew so I could not call for help. Could not call someone to lead me back to my house."

"I collapsed on the hard floor of the basement. I was exhausted and fell asleep until the morning. I woke up on that same floor my neck pinched from my awkward position. I made my way back up to the surface. Slowly, each step getting a full minute of pause. At the top. I found normalcy. My place…well the place I knew. Everything familiar including my phone. Outside, it was the right neighborhood."

"I locked the door to the basement. I blocked it with two chairs from the dining room. I chalked up the clothes in the dryer as a lost cause. The price to pay to stay in the right version of the world. I used a laundromat for the remaining months in that place. I never told the homeowner. I was sure they would never believe me."

Rudy waits until the redheaded girl indicates it is his turn again.

"One summer when I was in high school in Oregon, I worked at a gas station. This was back when in that state drivers could not pump their own gas. I was working with an older guy who got to stay inside where they sold snacks. I got to run out to each car and do the pumping. We had a freak thunderstorm, not something we usually had in June."

"A strange car pulled up, large built like a tank

but with no weaponry. I had never seen this make or model before. Looked like something built in Eastern Europe. The lettering on the side was strange too. At first, I thought maybe the words were in Cyrillic, but it was not that. The car was purely functional and ugly."

"Behind the wheel, an old man was staring straight ahead and not moving. He looked really old. When you are in high school, everyone over thirty looks ancient but I am pretty sure he was ancient. I thought he might be made of stone and not a real person at all. I tried to get his attention, to find out what he wanted, but he never moved. I was completely soaked by then. I got as close as I could. Through the back-seat driver-side door, I could hear something I did not expect to hear."

"I heard the sound of someone running in heavy shoes down a metallic staircase. On and on. There was a bit of a rise and drop in volume but overall getting louder. I imagined a spiral set of stairs winding around multiple times, multiple floors. The sound got louder and I prepared for, I don't know, something. I backed away from the door."

"The door behind the driver opened suddenly and a young man spilled out. He was out of breath and his hands were cupped together holding a pile of pieces of paper. He had a few feathers in his hair. Bright red and bright blue. He was very fair skinned. Not Native American"

He pushed the pile toward me and asked, "Will any of these work, to pay for fuel?"

I sorted through what turned out to be a wide variety of paper money. I saw currency from England, and China, and Japan. I also saw several that were for countries I had never heard of. I managed to pull out a few American bills of various denominations. Enough to pay for a full tank of unleaded. I turned toward the back of the vehicle and realized I had no idea how much gas it might take. I took a few more bills to be sure."

"When the gas tank would not take anymore, the vehicle drove off. The driver still statue-like. I should have taken some of the bills I could not identify. I realize now, a potential fortune had been put in front of me. The weather was so terrible that night that no other cars came in. I was able to spend most of my shift inside letting my clothes dry."

The redheaded girl smiles at Rudy, "That was much better."

Their posture worsens with each beer. They are both nearly parallel with the sofa cushions.

The redheaded girl straightens up and rises to unsteady feet. Her eyes are wide and bright like two candles.

She speaks without pause, staring at nothing. She says, "When they boarded up the houses when someone was sick the children cried, and the parents cried and everyone was hammering and pounding with their fists and with the flats of their hands like they were inside a coffin, but it was more like the cargo hold of a ship, the voyage was just a week or two, men with hard tiny black eyes spray-painted a number on the door, the number of souls inside the box, they said they will be back and they usually remembered to come back with a crowbar or an axe to see what subtraction must be done to the painted number."

Then her voice changes so that it sounds like a one-sided argument. The words are now in Mandarin Chinese, a language she does not speak. The words pass through her without understanding. Rudy does not know this language either.

"Then these men did the crying, in despair or in joy, more often a mixed tally, those sheets of plywood carried down the street felt like guillotines and nooses, those sheets held the line and did not negotiate."

The redheaded girl stops and realizes that she has made a mistake. She does not know where the words have come from. They do not feel like her words and are nothing that she could know.

There are too many beats of silence like listening to a record you don't know. Was that the last song? Or one more with a quiet, slow introduction?

Rudy gets to his feet. Four days of eating well and feeling strong.

He tells her, "I'm going to the store to get us some more beer."

She does not look up at him. She says, "You're not coming back, are you?"

He assures her, "No no nothing like that. I am…I'm just going to the store. I'll be back real quick."

As he walks out of the room, out of the house, out of her life, she says, "My name is Anastasia."

She does not feel her own forehead. Though the temptation is so strong. She knows she is on fire. She does not want to burn her hands.

"My name is Anastasia."

40 - The Song of Grendel's Mother

She is the fastest and strongest flyer.

She is the one to scout ahead. The one to be the intermediary between foraging efforts on the ground and hungry mouths in the tree.

She is faster every year. The babies do not age her wings. They have the opposite effect as if she is shedding the claims made by gravity.

And what babies she has made. Ones that screamed as she fed them until they matched her in size.

They have all left, except for the one with her now. He too will find a mate and roost elsewhere.

It is a pleasure to fly.

She memorizes the city. She can spot cats and raccoons. She senses the eagles and hawks that would take her from the sky.

Her sky.

They will never catch her.

Even as she reverses time to fly faster and longer, her mate tires and struggles to keep up. He is always somewhere behind her never alongside her.

So, she shares her food with him.

41 - The Moon is a Creature

Most of the houses that Rudy lives in have nothing remarkable to distinguish them. There are days when nothing happens, and he just survives.

He always finds the next empty place. He does not understand where the people have gone. Why the world is emptying out. He ricochets across the city. The strings of his paths forming a weave without pattern.

In the Proctor District, he finds a very old house with a front yard, overrun with weeds and blue wildflowers. The door opens easily so he locks it behind him.

All the furniture in the front room has been pushed up against the walls to clear a middle space. There he finds the remains of a fire. The partially burnt branches that are left behind are not familiar to him. They are not from trees or plants from the Pacific

Northwest. They did not burn all the way out to their tips and edges.

The off-white walls are covered with smoke stains all the way to the ceiling. Smeared fingerprints of air currents and vortices. All the windows are closed, and they have been nailed shut.

He finds many pairs of shoes encircling the fire remnant, still laced and belted. They are pointed toward the center. Sneakers and fancy Italian shoes and sandals and boots and platform heels.

Beyond the circle of shoes, he stumbles across a book on the floor. The heavy hardcover volume has no words on the cover, just an embossed image of the solar system, but only out to Mars, the fourth planet.

On the title page inside, he reads *"Revolutionary Discoveries in the Composition and Nature of Solar System Bodies"* by the Pierce County Planetary Revisionist Society.

He carries the book towards the dining room table where he can sit and read. The table is covered in a pile of smoke detectors with the wiring cut and batteries removed.

There is handwriting in the margins of every page with different colored ink in various levels of readability. Near the front, he finds a yellow page inserted with only a few lines on it.

> *Mars is a graveyard*
> *for the skeletons of men*
> *who arrived with coins in their teeth*
> *and no shoes on their feet.*

The book holds equations and recipes and rituals and maps and the detailed descriptions of plants from all over the world. Parts of the book are in Arabic. Parts of it are in French. Other parts are in languages he cannot identify.

There are six pages that are just unknown symbols with no cipher included. Rudy counts 172 different symbols on these pages.

Another section is called *"The Other Way to Mars"* though it reads more like a recipe and less like directions for travel. The ingredients call for specific branches of trees from different continents and a list of possible coins that are considered acceptable. The further he reads, the recipe evolves into more of a spell.

The book has no table of contents, so he just works methodically through the book from the beginning to the end. He skips the sections that he cannot read.

The schematics of the solar system do not make sense to him. There are too many planets. Two more than he knows. They are not named but designated as numbered objects 529 and 1003. Later in the book, both of these objects are listed with a series of words: a name in English, a Cyrillic word, some Chinese characters. Perhaps competing candidates for an official name. These planets are placed further out from the sun than Neptune.

Pluto has been written over in a thick black marker. Like a face crossed out or obscured out of anger in a high school yearbook. But a new picture of Pluto, slightly smaller, has been taped over the black spot. A rectangle cut from a different book. A transfusion of foreign paper and incompatible ink.

One section of the book seems to have silver and pink glitter embedded in the pages. The header of the section is titled *"Biological Selenology."* Alongside, these typed words are cursive ones in calligraphy quality handwriting.

"The moon is a creature."

The pages that follow outline the biology and anatomy of the moon. The author is confident in his theory and includes no indication of humor or irony. The chapter references the works of others including two Chinese names who have researched the multiple growth stages of the moon, and an Egyptian selenologist who studied the moon's life processes. These processes do not much resemble digestion or respiration. There are schematic blueprints of the passage of the moon through space. Where the author should say "orbits," they instead describe "tunnels."

For hours, Rudy ignores the growling of his stomach. But he cannot ignore the arrival of night. He has spent the entirety of the day sitting at the table going through the book.

He surveys the rest of the house. There is no power due to some savage cutting of the wiring at the breaker box. The air is stagnant from the sealed windows. There is no food of any kind. There is no running water.

He waits through the night in the dark unable to read more of the book.

He leaves in the morning to find a new place. The only thing worth salvaging is the book. It is too heavy and unwieldy to carry. He leaves it behind and heads south.

42 - The Song of Lazarus

Lazarus can see the wing that should be there.

A mirror image of the other, flawless and elegant like that of his traveling companions.

He does not see the one that is actually there, pointed the wrong way. He uses the one that should be to fly.

Take off your glasses and he is beautiful. He is the envy of all gravity bound creatures. He is the defiance of heaviness. He is an impulsive change of direction. He is an escape hatch, a trap door, a fast train out of town.

Lazarus still finds meals on the roads. Those death currents that deposit riches but ask a toll. A low percentage sacrifice.

The current went for him one day when he was slow.

Very few live to see two days of being slow.

He had hopped when he should have flown. He was scavenging solo when he should have relied on a lookout.

He has survived the death swipe. Now he is stronger. His legs feel as invulnerable and solid as the sidewalk. His claws as hard as that of a small hawk. He does not tire easily. When the others are sleeping, he is alert. A sentry waiting for the sun.

He decides that he will not die. That he will not stop like all the others have, and all the others will do.

He will defy. He will teach the children of the children of the children of his companions.

He will defy.

The good wing allows Lazarus to travel in space and time forward as normal. But the other wing, the broken one, the one that is pointed the wrong way, sends him laterally perhaps even a bit backward chronologically. It keeps him young. He does not progress in age. He is cheating death.

Ghost wing. Wraith wing. Spirit wing. One is for the eyes, and one is for the wind. One does all the work. Lazarus has a wing in two worlds.

43 - Again We Meet for the First Time

Rudy's backpack is getting light, which is a bad sign. He needs to find a new place to stay. A new place to stock up on rations.

He searches for indications or clues for the next place. If there is some equivalent of the old hobo secret language of symbols to mark safe houses, he is unaware. There might be patterns in the graffiti or carved in the moss, but nothing he can read.

He hears the rumbling of an idling diesel engine. He recognizes the man in the driver's seat of a large pickup truck. A solid sunburnt man with a baseball hat.

"Hello Harvey," Rudy calls out.

The man in the truck turns to Rudy and responds, "Do I know you?"

"A few months back we hung out for a week or so."

Rudy's brain whispers something relevant in his ear. "Oh yeah, you have that living out a sequence thing going on for you. So I guess that has not happened yet for you. When we met then, you already knew me, and you apologized for something."

Harvey smiles, "It seems you do know me. One of the benefits of this life is I never meet any strangers. One of us always knows the other. So again, we meet for the first time. And you are…"

"Rudy. My name is Rudy. Are you still living in that home out by Point Defiance?"

Harvey says, "Actually, no. But I guess I could ask you the right questions and learn what I'm going to do next." He opens the passenger door. "Get in. I'm living with a nurse in the Stadium district. And yes, we are a thing. She does not believe in the weird time thing. She has that science background, so she pokes holes in the logic. I just put up my hands in surrender. I tell her I don't understand either. It's just the way. I didn't choose it. I have never received any useful instructions."

They drive across town through light traffic. Harvey cannot get the truck down some of the narrower streets, so they have to park several blocks away and walk to the house.

As they approach the rambler, a woman in pink and blue medical scrubs opens the screen door. Her dark hair is pulled back in a ponytail. She smiles at Harvey but then notices Rudy. She pats her left palm twice over her chin and mouths the word "mask."

Harvey smiles. "He's fine. Trust me. This is Rudy. He is staying for dinner. Rudy, this is Zee. She is going to scowl at you, and she won't hug you, but she is a life-saving angel. Works up at St. Joe's."

Dinner is hot dogs barbecued in the backyard. Two for each of them with mustard and grilled onions. Rudy is never asked what he wanted on his hot dogs. Some macaroni salad out of a plastic circular container from a local supermarket. Ice water with lemon slices.

Rudy explains some history. "I hung out with Harvey before and took him to the hospital when he got really sick. I guess you don't know about that."

Harvey says, "News to me." He puts up his hands. "I will pretend to be surprised when it happens."

Zee stares at Rudy. "So you're in on this little backward time game too?" She turns to Harvey. "Should we go through this again? How it falls apart when you look at it closely?"

Harvey says, "No. You win. You are right. You have logically proven this bumblebee is too big to fly. This bumblebee will therefore stop its flying in accordance with that conclusion."

Harvey and Zee make up a spare room for Rudy.

Rudy asks, "Do you have anything to read? I don't really sleep."

Zee asks, "You mean you have insomnia?"

"No, I don't sleep. I have not slept in over a year and a half."

Zee responds, "Well that's impossible. You could do that for a few days but nothing long-term. You'd be seeing all sorts of things that are not there. You would be crazy by now. That is even sillier than that backward time thing. I guess I understand why you two are friends. Let me grab some paperbacks. I hope you like science fiction."

Zee brings him a stack of old books that smell

like even older libraries. During the night, he works through *The Day of the Triffids* by John Wyndham and *The Lathe of Heaven* by Ursula K. LeGuin.

In another room, Zee asks Harvey for more information on Rudy.

"Honestly, I don't know anything. I have never met him before today."

Zee pushes Harvey hard with a two-hand shove. "You asshole. You know he says he never sleeps. Did you know that?"

In the morning. Zee finds Rudy sitting on his bed with the sheets and blankets completely undisturbed. He has finished two books and is starting *Red Planet* by Robert A. Heinlein.

"You really didn't sleep at all? Not even a cat nap?" Rudy shakes his head. "Maybe I could take you with me to the hospital. Get you checked out. They could help you get back to normal."

Rudy says, "I appreciate the offer, but I would prefer not to. That is not the best thing for me. It is hard to explain, but I just ask that you trust me."

Zee says, "Sleep deprivation is no minor thing. Are you taking any drugs or medication to keep you awake?"

"Nothing. Caffeine was not helpful. I just...don't close my eyes anymore."

Two more days pass in a similar manner. Rudy eats well and reads the stack of old science fiction novels. He catches up on laundry. He travels with Harvey during the day, loading boxes into the truck and making deliveries.

44 - We Live on the Rooftop

Harvey gives this spiel while driving. Rudy listens with his head turned toward the driver to hear over the raindrops hitting the windshield.

"The largest mass of life on the planet is not animal or plant. It is the fungal kingdom. The majority of this is underground. Under our feet, under our roads, under our floors. When you think of fungi and maybe you don't, you think of mushrooms and truffles and strange shapes attached to the sides of trees. But these are just the tips of the thing, the fruiting bodies they call them. These are just masks and false faces. Probes, watchers, scouts. There is a network of organic cables burrowing through the soil and even piercing harder materials. They run for miles. These cables share information, and they share nutrients. The network even extends into plants, especially the trees. They can say this tree needs some specific nutrients or they can announce the imminent passing of an unhealthy tree."

"But the fungal kingdom is not entirely altruistic. Some of these fungi reach up through the individual trees, under the bark, like under the skin. So many fingers reaching for the sky. There are fungal entities that span acres hidden from the sun. And it feeds and it drains, and it grows. I don't think the trees are their friends, I think they are the livestock. The fungal kingdom breaks down the things that die. They come in after the predators, and after the scavengers have had their courses. They dissolve and they clean. When we withhold our dead from their process, when we place them in tightly sealed boxes or when we cremate our loved ones, we have prevented the fungal kingdom from harvesting us. We have interrupted the loop."

"The fungal kingdom is a giant filter feeder. Sitting at the bottom of the world. Collecting all that decay. Like a giant whale with its tail heated by the hot core of the Earth and its mouth full of baleen, grinning in the dirt. The fungi have no bones, so it erases itself from the fossil record. An invisible hand in history."

"So, we are not the dominant form of life on the planet. We do not live in the great house of the world. The fungal kingdom lives in that house, and we live on the rooftop. Mankind and the other surface dwellers are just inconsequential beasts. Living on that roof thinking we run this place."

45 - Cavalry

Zee comes home from the hospital with a passenger in her car. The newcomer is taller than Rudy wearing light blue scrubs. He is a Black man with short, cropped hair. He is wider than Rudy or Harvey. He is wearing a mask, the same color as his scrubs.

He is a fellow nurse named Danny Winfield. He has a voice that is gentle and methodical and lower than seems possible.

When Rudy steps forward to shake his hand, Danny steps backward, instinctively. He says, "Not doing that. We gotta be careful. I don't want to give you anything and I don't want you to give me anything."

Harvey makes cheeseburgers. Everyone gets two and they are devoured before they can get cold. Zee has changed out of her scrubs into a t-shirt and jeans. They eat outside in the backyard sitting in lawn chairs. They are spaced far apart from each other.

Everyone but Danny has to shout to be heard.

When Harvey asks how the day went, Zee puts up a right hand and drops her chin. "People getting sick. People dying. I don't want to talk about it."

After sunset they all go back into the house. Danny puts his mask back on.

Zee puts on a record with a bright red cover. The songs are mostly instrumental: saxophone and tuba and intricate drumming. She tells Rudy that the band is called Sons of Kemet. She tells him that they are the best band on the planet. She corrects herself, "Galaxy, think galaxy."

Rudy does not notice when Harvey says to Zee, "We are going to need this to be a little louder." He turns the volume knob clockwise.

Rudy is sitting in the middle of the couch, enjoying the music. He notices that Danny is now standing. He sees that Harvey is also standing.

Zee addresses Rudy, "You know you are our friend, and you know what I do. I am a nurse. I save people. I keep them alive. Danny and I do that every day. What you were doing is not sustainable. Sleep is an important part of your health. Not sleeping is a surefire way to go crazy. We have to fix this. We are here to fix this. We don't take an oath like the doctors, but we live it more."

Danny nods in agreement.

"You need to know I only want what is best for you. I would never hurt you. This is a sort of intervention."

Zee takes a hypodermic needle out of her bag. "This will help you sleep. It will make you sleep immediately, and you need that, no matter what you think. So. Will you let me do this?"

Rudy gets to his feet and says, "No, that will kill me."

"This will not kill you. This is just a needle. Like getting a flu shot or drawing blood. I'm very good at this."

Then Danny and Harvey are on either side of Rudy, each grabbing an arm. He notices that Danny has put on latex gloves. The trio of large men collapses onto the couch, which becomes very crowded. Rudy resists and struggles against his captors.

Harvey is hard muscle and Rudy throws him off the couch.

Danny is soft muscle. He absorbs impact and gives no ground.

Danny speaks in a steady litany. "It is going to be all right. Trust us. We are your friends."

His rumbling voice locks in with the tuba on the record. Harvey returns to re-grip Rudy's left arm. He uses his weight to keep Rudy sitting down.

Zee yells "Dammit Harvey, can't you control him?"

Harvey says, "He's too strong and he's panicking. He's gone wild."

Danny is still laying down a bassline. "Stop your struggling. Time to sleep. You need the peace."

Zee watches the struggle, hoping to find a moment where she can get a safe shot at one of Rudy's arms.

Rudy yells, "If I sleep, I won't wake up. You have to believe me. I'm not crazy. For me, sleep means I die. You don't want to do this. You don't want this on your hands, and I am not ready to die."

Zee yells back, "You'll sleep like a baby and you'll feel so much better. You'll get a full night's rest."

Then there are two distinct sounds. Two knocks on the door. Thump. Thump. Everyone stops.

Zee turns towards the door as do the men. She puts the needle on the counter and walks to the door.

Rudy pleads, "Don't open the door. Don't let it in. It will be the end of me and probably the end of you too."

Zee opens the door and there is nobody there. She looks down and sees two marbles on the front porch. She looks up.

It comes in like a funnel made of black tar, made of crude oil. But it is all feathers and sharp edges. It is the sound of day creatures who need space to maneuver. They have braved the night into this small space.

The funnel makes a variety of sounds. There is the sound of a cat meowing. The sound of a raven croaking. There is the sound of children screaming. There is a mechanical sound.

Hands go to faces, to protect from the storm inside as the crows pinwheel like biplanes in a cave.

Rudy is released by Harvey and Danny. He runs out the front door before any words are spoken. A few seconds later, six crows become a tail streaming behind him. He is careful not to step on the two marbles by the front door.

One of the marbles is a cat's eye, staring up at the melee. The other is clear and gray like a scaled down crystal ball for a clairvoyant rat.

46 - Dusted in Your Own Feathers

"Your hair is unkempt. You look like a hermit. You look like a hobo, a messiah. You are an arrest waiting to happen."

On the street corner, this stranger pulls out scissors from a holster somewhere.

She is too short, so she pushes him to the ground. She spins around him. Clip clip. He has ears again.

She smells like acetone. She smells like hair dye. He closes his eyes to avoid elbows and to not stare at her chest. Her knee is in his ribs to stabilize her balance. She climbs over him. The scissors move fast and often. The most delicate of cuts.

"My name is Thao and I own my own salon. You have not been there. It is full of old ladies."

She is dancing alone as he is paralyzed.

"They used to have us practice on homeless men. You appear to have a home. Well fed, and decently adorned. But your locks are untended. You have no barber and no hairdresser and obviously no woman to tell you how you look."

One hand holds, positions itself, while the other does the cutting. A vice and a blade. She is not that different from a butcher. He feels himself being whittled down to something more presentable. Something to put on the counter, in the display window.

Thao pulls a cell phone out of her pocket and presses a few buttons to make it play music. Rudy hears Debbie Harry's voice.

"There. You hold this since you are not much good at talking. Lower. Out of the way. In your hands in your lap."

Sometimes she sings along, but mostly she clips to the beat of the drums. In time with Clem Burke.

This would be easier with some water. She is a blur. She is a flash.

Five songs in and she is sweaty. He can trace her winding around him by the drops of perspiration hitting his face and his neck. His eyes are closed, but he is in no danger of falling asleep.

She is not perfect with the sharp edges. He gets poked, but not enough to draw blood. She is less accurate with her rounder edges. He gets jarred by hips and chest like an unwilling dance partner.

When the last song on the Blondie album completes, she is done trimming his hair. A dance and a soundtrack of the exact same length.

"Open your eyes. No more danger."

Thao steps back two paces and walks around him. Inspecting her work.

"You're even prettier than I thought." She wipes sweat from her face onto her shirt. "If I didn't have a…" She flicks her right middle finger twice on the wedding band on her left ring finger. "Well, you wouldn't be getting any sleep tonight."

Rudy says, "I have not slept in two years."

"Don't tempt me like that."

She holsters her shears somewhere not obvious. "I'm afraid I've left you a bit of a mess. You are dusted in your own feathers. Take a shower. Wash your clothes. Go find someone half as gorgeous as me and call it a win."

She collects her phone from his hands. She takes his picture before he knows it. Before he can pose or protest.

"I do want to make sure you have a roof and something to eat."

Rudy answers, " I have a place. I will be fine."

Thao says, "And so will I. It's been a pleasure."

47 - Prelude to a Dog's Honeymoon

There is a park on a short sleeve, no-jacket summer morning where people do not mix. They exist as satellites, undersea mines, separate asteroids, leaving space for each other. Objects avoiding collision.

There is a bench that can hold three people who are sitting down or one person who is lying down sleeping. Rudy sits on one end of this bench. His hair follicles are each pointed at different stars that are invisible in the midday sun. But they are still there. They do not sleep.

He should hold a book or a picnic lunch. But his hands just rest on his knees.

A young woman chooses the other end of the bench. She has fair skin and phantom light blue eyes. Her ancestors did not see the sun for months at a time. Lightly toned eyes did not squint while staring at hills of snow. Her arms are bare and likely to catch fire if she stays out more than thirty minutes.

Her hair is light brown, a compromise on the possible range. It is not homogenous. It is beef broth, glacier melt, the bark of ancient trees.

They sit like this in silence for ten minutes then fifteen. The meter on her exposure to solar radiation is winding down.

She slips into a smile easily. The tracks on her face, the evidence of her frequent laughter, have arrived a decade early.

"I would like to talk to you, but we need to move over there." She points to a different bench in the shade of an oak tree. Without waiting for a response, she walks to that bench.

Rudy follows. Despite his long strides from being a foot taller than her, he has to set a good pace to keep up. She sits in the middle of the bench.

She has a bag slung over her shoulder and it may as well be an infinite purse. For it does hold a picnic lunch, multiple books, and several unidentified things that clank and echo off each other.

The lunch is a sandwich, ham and cheese on wheat with mayonnaise and mustard. She demonstrates that they will trade bites. He takes conservative bites, so he does not eat more than his share.

Then an apple is shared the same way until the core is tossed into a nearby garbage can.

She pulls out a large water bottle to chase the food. Again, far too big to be hidden in her bag. She is accurate and true in her retrieval of whatever she wants. There is no rummaging or searching for the next thing.

"Tell your friends that I am not dangerous.

That you are safe with me." She tells him. "They do not need to worry."

"I don't have any friends here."

"Those friends. Two on the ground and one in the tree." She aims her index finger at each of the crows. "If I feed them, maybe they'll be friends of mine too."

She grabs a small package of saltine crackers from that bag whose outer dimensions show no change. She whips three of the rectangular crackers like shuriken into the area just outside of shadow the tree. Each crow collects their own cracker.

"My name is Freya. I may change it someday. If you have any suggestions, I am taking notes." She taps on the front cover of a small journal that is now in her hands.

"My name is Rudy. And those are Garfield and Arlene." The two crows start making meowing sounds and bowing in synchronization at the cracker provider.

"And this is Lazarus." The third crow with a left wing made of bad geometry, but functionally fine, lands on the uninhabited end of the bench.

"I was going to read this afternoon." She holds up a copy of *The Grapes of Wrath* by John Steinbeck with several bookmarks sticking out of it. The cover is partially handmade illustrated in watercolors. Rudy suspects the watercolors are also somewhere in the bag.

Instead, they talk and talk without clear direction or purpose.

She tells them that no one's ears hold up well under close visual scrutiny. They are all out of place with the rest of the features of the face. The best way to get over an ex is to repeatedly review photographs of their ears. Soon you will find it impossible to understand why you had given your heart to them.

He tells her the story of how he met the trio of crows and the other trio that is foraging elsewhere. Without the clear context, his narration could be about six of his human friends.

Freya reminds herself that Lazarus is a crow. That Bowie is a crow. Somehow Grendel's Mother is a crow.

Two hours go by, and they are still conversing. Instead of going to a movie, they have talked all the way through it.

She faces him and makes sure he knows that he has been seen.

She says, "Here is what we should do. We should get a room, just the two of us and there should be no phones and no televisions and no radios. A locked door. Neither of us should speak at all in kindness or in anger or in humor or in pleasure. Neither of us should make any noise."

"We should be without clothes. And with love. And spend the day just eating and sleeping and fucking and sleeping. I offer this to you. As many days of this as you can handle and as you can stand."

"I offer you a dog's honeymoon," as she moves her hand as if to reveal or unveil a grand gift.

He smiles back at her. He thinks of a longer more romantic answer but just says, "Yes."

They get snacks from a convenience store. Cookies and candy and beef jerky and potato chips and soda. Two children turned loose with allowance money. Salt and sugar. Colors in the candy that you do not find naturally in the world. Road trip food.

She pays for the room. There is a wallet in that bag too.

As they walk down the hallway to their room, she says, "We will stay until we run out of money. We will stay until we run out of food. And maybe a little past that. Until they kick us out. Until we are tired of each other. Until the sight of each other's ears is too much. Until my skin becomes allergic to your skin or vice versa. Until we need to go outside and make sure the world has not collapsed or vanished in our absence. While that is unlikely, it is possible because we were not there to watch it. To stop it."

From a housekeeping cart in the hotel hallway, she steals extra supplies. She laterals several rolls of toilet paper to him like footballs. He throws them deep into the room. She grabs an extra stack of towels and chases him into the room.

Then they close the door behind them. Hermetically sealed off from the rest of the world.

48 - The Song of Garfield and Arlene

Garfield chose Arlene because she is the bravest hawk chaser even when it is not her egg on the nest.

Arlene chose Garfield because of his song.

Garfield chose Arlene after watching her pursue and spear dragonflies midair with their purple thin wings.

Arlene chose Garfield because his voice imitates that of a predatory neighborhood cat which he uses to scare away and confuse larger creatures.

Arlene chose Garfield because he taught her his song.

Garfield chose Arlene because her version of the song was more convincing.

Arlene chose Garfield for the way he sits on a rooftop and announces the start of the day.

Arlene chose Garfield because he is bold and can wait till the last few seconds to avoid fast cars with a few graceful crow hops.

Garfield chose Arlene because he intends to build a family of false felines to drive the real ones away.

Arlene chose Garfield because he knows the specific throat sound that indicates everything, all of the world, all that can be traveled to.

Arlene chose Garfield because he uses this sound when he calls to her.

Garfield chose Arlene because she slows down time.

Arlene chose Garfield because he is an endless source of noise, a river of croaks and meows and screeches and clicks.

Garfield chose Arlene because she is not afraid of the wind and the rain at night.

49 - Dog's Honeymoon

Freya sleeps like the dead, and she sleeps like the newly born, and she sleeps like someone who has no ghosts and no pursuers. She sleeps like someone who has no guilt and no envy. Someone who is not worried about tomorrow's meal. Beside her, Rudy does not sleep.

The dog's honeymoon is not the reprieve he was hoping for. He cannot, will not, fall asleep and does not even close his eyes.

He thinks about how he got here. He wonders why Freya chose him. He is not in control of his path.

His mouth tastes like gauze and industrial cleaner. A sterile feeling. He feels her heartbeat in her wrist and through her skull resting on his chest. He untangles the syncopation to find his own heart's cadence. His is more muffled and slower, almost reptilian.

She numbs different parts of him as she shifts in sleep. His right arm is asleep now making other parts, including his brain, envious. The arm is anesthetized, ready for surgery. He tries not to wake her.

She has tattoos. Everyone in Tacoma has some except him.

There is a young woman who is not Freya on her upper left arm. She is in a small boat up near the prow. She is holding a sword in the air like a beacon. The boat has a single small rectangular sail which does not look sufficient to travel on the ocean. The woman on her arm has extra eyes. Three extra in fact. Rudy does not ask about the eyes.

It is a tremendous amount of detail to be displayed on a small bicep. If he had a magnifying glass, would the resolution bring out even more detail. What is in the water alongside the boat? What is the color of the woman's eyes? Are they all the same color? Does the woman on the boat have a tattoo? Is that tattoo of Freya?

The days in the hotel room go by very slowly. He is forgetting the sound of her voice. He likes her voice. Her sense of timing. Her strange choice of words.

He has had many questions to ask but cannot ask them.

What is her full name? How old is she? Where does she work? What about her family? Where has she lived? Why are her toenails painted ten different colors? Are he and Freya the last humans? Are they working diligently to repopulate the planet?

He has much he wants to tell her, including how he got here. Perhaps he has willingly sacrificed his voice. An unclearly stated deal. By agreeing, did he give up speech?

He is abiding by the terms of the offer. His experience is partial as he cannot partake in the sleeping portion, the rest and recuperation part.

The room is white. The curtains are white, and the sheets are white, and the bedspread is white, and the walls are white. However, the carpet has an ugly brown and orange pattern. It looks like something that is much older than could be possible, much older than the planet. A part of your body that was aged and wrinkled before you were even born.

They have worked their way deep into the cache of snacks. He purposely chooses only the protein and savory snacks.

They are in the cabin of a ship crossing the Pacific. They are in the sterilized chamber of a spacecraft, heading toward a distant star. They are disobeying time and will arrive naked and young and beautiful under different skies.

They are memorizing each other's bodies. They are counting ribs and counting freckles. He writes her name, Freya, like the Norse goddess, on the palm of his hand using his finger and no ink. He is reminding himself, grounding himself, with a few facts so he does not lose everything. He has lost time. He has lost speech and hearing. He has given away the world, except for her.

He is missing his crow companions. Their caws and squawks are comforting sounds like crashing waves for someone who lives by the ocean.

She gropes around for his hand while she sleeps. He unclasps her fingers so he can walk to the bathroom.

He walks on the balls of his feet ninja style to not wake her. She deserves all aspects of the dog's honeymoon.

As he crosses the room naked, he thinks of another nude procession. That one down a street, under a faint sun, when he was bleeding and torn. There are no ants to guide his feet now.

In the bathroom, he taps his fingernails gently on the marble countertop. Trying to make sure his ears still work. A method of sensory calibration. He does not hear trucks or sirens outside. He does not hear anyone walking in the hallway. No voices and no babies screaming,

They have built a mound of used towels. Some are not fit for future use. He will need to pilfer from the maid's cart again. Yesterday he negotiated in pantomime silence with a woman twice his age. He made gestures to indicate a trade of the white cotton towel wrapped around his waist for one from her trolley. She hid her smile under her hand and offered him three. When he turned back to the room, he had dropped his towel before leaving the hallway. It was only fair to meet the terms of the agreement.

The fluids on his body are partially his. The foreign ones left under permission and affection.

In the mirror, he sees he is breaking out in red splotches across his chest where Freya's head has been resting. The drool from her deep slumber is reacting on his chest, burrowing through his skin. Or maybe he is just allergic to the hotel soap.

When he returns to the bed, she is awake and writing in a small notebook. She does not show him what she is writing. She does not use the journal to pass notes and messages. She closes the notebook and places it on the nightstand.

Then she flips him on to his back and is on top

of him. They move together in silence for several minutes.

She changes her pace, shifts to a lower gear. She makes two fists at the height of her shoulders, her head tilts so that she is pointed at the ceiling. Her face tightens and Rudy no longer recognizes her. When she speaks, she is loud and shrill, like a frightened horse. Rudy does not know this voice.

"Before the plague, before the masks, I was a Norse goddess who crossed the pond and then a continent to be here in Tacoma. A woman with a sword in a boat. Before the plague, before the masks, I would greet friends and newly made acquaintances with the two kisses on the cheek, European style. If I kissed you on the cheek, I had your allegiance from that point on. They don't let you carry a sword on the Amtrak trains, so I slummed it on the Greyhound buses. I kept the sword in my lap. The empty seat next to me stayed empty. But my passport doesn't mention anything about anywhere in Scandinavia. It says Cork, Ireland as place of birth and as place of residence. I did not lose the sword on the journey. I gave it away. I recognized someone who needed it more. I have never second-guessed this decision. I learned to be a dental hygienist. I spend my days talking to people who have various instruments deep in their mouth. These are lopsided conversations with no responses to my questions. One day at the end of a cleaning session, an old man listed off all his answers. All thirty of them in proper sequence to everything I had asked. My days are full of my voice and the sounds of drills and cleaners and x-ray machines. I always wear a mask. Men and some women get lost in my focused eyes. They seem to say, 'I will follow you into the ocean. Don't ask me to follow you into the ocean.' I stay fair skinned and pale by working inside. The woman with the sword on the boat is hidden under my sleeve. I dream of a day that is quiet, without my own voice, without machinery, without water pumps. I think I could be quiet and peaceful for maybe forty days. When I introduce myself, I say I am Freya, like the Norse goddess. And they will think that I am too small to carry a sword."

Freya stops talking and she stops moving. She clutches her mouth like it is not hers to control. She dismounts though neither of them has finished.

The commotion of the world returns. The chaos. The cacophony. The sounds that are not silence and not music. There are car door slams and angry horns and alarms.

Two sets of little feet pad heavily down the hallway outside the room. Beyond the airlock. Heavier feet are in pursuit.

He can hear the small room refrigerator changing gears. The air conditioner struggling to keep pace with its task.

A voice accompanying some knocks on the door. "Are you all right in there? Are you still alive? Can I bring you anything."

Through the wall on one side of the room, Rudy hears a loud television with the evening news on. Through the opposite wall, a couple argues though the words are unclear. All the noises have accumulated for three days and now are released.

Rudy could tell her that she is beautiful. She probably is beautiful. That he will protect her from monsters and pain and all who would harm her. He could offer all that he has, which is nearly nothing. A wanderer's life. Outrunning death.

So, he offers her nothing and he does not ask all the questions he has listed in his head during the past three days. Her outburst was like the manic speech of the six men in the church courtyard. Like the rant of the redheaded girl that evolved into Chinese. He takes this an early warning system announcing the one who chases him.

He decouples her fate from his as he leaves. He feels her touch on his left forearm. The Norse goddess has left five small red circles behind. They will pulse from her distant attention and her thoughts. They will stay there and blink like phosphorescent creatures on the ocean floor for three more days.

In the maple tree out in front of the hotel, two crows wait for him. Garfield and Arlene bow in sync to him. He thinks three days have passed, but with the curtains drawn, he is not entirely sure. They have been living outside of time. Perhaps forty days have gone by. He has reached the other side of Pacific. He has arrived on a different planet to stare up at a different star. Had they brought enough food to last forty days?

In truth, it has only been three days. Another three will pass before the red spots on his arm will vanish entirely.

50 - Grendel Deserves a Song But Does Not Have One

Grendel deserves a song but does not have one.

He is still young and maybe a song is yet to arrive. He could steal or permute one from the other five.

Grendel does not do that.

Some days, most days, he tries on silence to see if this is a good coat. He is a stealth bird who just materializes. This is his un-song.

But the sound builds up over days and can no longer be contained in his body. The pressure feels digestive and it feels inevitable.

Then Grendel is the loudest thing. His voice is the end of song and the end of silence. One morning, he turned his body and his head and his wings to point in the direction of a rooster who had announced the dawn. Like a weathervane spun by the call and not by the wind. He unleashed in that direction. A distorted inorganic roar that pegs all the gauges.

The rooster stopped at that moment and skipped the next day. Which meant the sun almost skipped the next day too.

Grendel's Mother scolded him after that. Again, he was just a child who did not know how to navigate while away from a safe nest. He listened and offered no rebuttal.

Many people in Tacoma have chickens in their backyard, primarily for the daily supply of inexpensive eggs. However, roosters are not allowed in the city limits. Roosters are outlaws which means they are rare but not imaginary.

To sound that morning alarm is a big risk. It draws the attention of neighbors who want more hours of sleep. Their tolerance may be purchased in eggs. The call also draws the attention of raccoons.

Grendel deserves a song, but he does not have one yet. All sound is either music or silence or noise. He oscillates between the last two.

To select the quiet is to choose austerity. To be an observer, a watcher, a listener.

To select noise is to blast a hole through the sky. To descend down a tunnel of disorienting dissonance.

To drive others away. To scare away your prey. To announce the ending of the world every day until finally does it end.

Grendel takes it as a challenge. He listens to the mechanical creatures in the world. The ones on the ground who punish and finish other creatures, even sometimes his fellow crows. The ones high in the sky that interrupt the sun. If he can keep growing, beyond the size of the ravens, beyond the size of the eagles, he could be louder than any of those beasts.

The noise from Grendel is that un-song, that ur-song. The sound you don't hear with your ears, but with your fingers and your toes. The noise is a very old concoction from the time before there were crows, before there were birds. It has been lifted and borrowed. It is subterranean fault lines slamming into each other, then pitch shifted poorly until its beauty and patterns are lost.

51 – Blast Radius

Rudy finds himself shepherded in a specific direction while wandering in a neighborhood. He avoids street corners where angry people argue, where dogs growl. He avoids streets so dark he would not know if someone was alongside him until he was grabbed.

He remembers this street and this block, though he was only here once. In that house across the street, his fortune had been foretold, more specifically his death.

He crosses the street as though drawn by a gravitational pole or magnetism or nostalgia, or unanswered questions, or even doubt of his own memory. Something other than a choice.

There is no car in the driveway. No lights on inside the house.

A window on the side of the house is partially open. He uses that to enter. He has become very skilled at getting into buildings unseen.

Inside, the place is nearly empty. Skeptical and a bit reckless, he flips on a light switch. He is overwhelmed by the yellowish white walls with no pictures and no artwork. Just several nail holes where something decorative was hung. For furniture, there are a few small generic tables and nothing else. Nothing of value. The house is quiet like a park after a late night snowfall.

The refrigerator is empty except for a box of baking soda but is still running.

He walks into the bedroom, the center of the galaxy. That light switch still works too. Another room nearly cleaned out. There is a bedframe, which holds a boxspring, but no mattress. There is a nightstand next to the bedframe with two drawers. Stained reddish wood and polished brass handles.

There is no good reason to open that top drawer, but he does so slowly. It may be a trap.

The deck of cards he remembers is centered in the drawer. Around the cards in a perfect circle is a perimeter of dead black ants. They are not pointed outward as if they were guarding the deck. They are pointed inward as if they were approaching it carefully. Tiptoeing a sneak attack. Their deaths were slow and nuclear. They did not complete their mission.

He closes the drawer. He decides to leave.

He finds no name on the mailbox. That would have been too easy. He walks away with no clues of her identity. No evidence of her existence. No proof of her being alive or dead.

The six crows are in a hawthorn tree across the street. They are completely silent and still. He can spot them easily now. They do not come to him, so he crosses the street between cars.

The full moon is not the same to Rudy on this clear night. He watches closely, trying to distinguish movement on its surface.

He wants to call it out and say I do not trust you. But he stays quiet. He does not want to draw attention from an entity like that. He does not want to be the crazy man spotted from bedroom windows as he points at and scolds a reflective white object in the sky. The moon may just be another sentry. Another lookout. The crow high in the trees telling the others where to go.

52 - The Feeding Habits of Blackberry Bushes

Rudy is thinking about Freya. He is wondering if he did her wrong by running away and leaving her.

Did he lead death away from her to protect her or did he leave her unguarded?

He has already lost the sound of her voice. There were too many days when he did not hear it. He tries to remember how she smelled, but he only recalls the citrus and coconut combination of the hotel soap and shampoo that coated both of them.

Rudy is on auto pilot. Just enough attention to keep from falling down on the sidewalk. He thinks that he is tired of running. Even when he is standing still, he is still running. When he is doing nothing, he is running.

He wishes he could sleep. He has covered so many miles on foot in Tacoma that his feet hardly need shoes anymore. They are like the heavy thick pads of some large carnivorous mammal.

His clothing is patchwork. He is a composite man. Everything he is wearing, was once worn by another man. From a closet in some abandoned house.

The shirt is from a house in the Proctor neighborhood. Someone who had a cat. The jacket, the veteran of his wardrobe, goes back to a place in Hilltop. Despite the months of continual use, it hangs on to the fine hairs of a dog's undercoat. Maybe a German Shepherd. Two household pets meet for the first time on his body, forced into proximity and travel.

The pants are dress trousers. Thick material for fine restaurants and board meetings.

But he notices a worn spot on the right knee. Based on the unflawed condition of the rest of the pants, this was not from accumulated wear, but from a traumatic event. He is wearing the evidence of another man's injuries. One that left a skinned knee or a purple and orange hematoma. The pants were padding, but not armor.

The shoes are too big. They are expensive and made in Italy. The high-quality soles protect his feet from the repeated impact on pavement. His toes, however, bounce around in the extra space and suffer loudly.

His feet are swaddled in dark socks. These are swapped out the most frequently even more than the underwear which are white cotton briefs.

He cycles out his garments like a snake molting. The shed skin is faded and shrunken. No use for anyone. For a time, his coloring is bold again and everything is clean.

Rudy has lost everything a few times now. Stripped of all belongings and clothes in the church courtyard. He left behind a well-stocked backpack at Zee and Harvey's place after his rescue by the crows.

In his strides, in his pounding of heels and toes on the sidewalk he loses himself and loses focus. He is not daydreaming. It is something else.

As Rudy opens his mind to the history of these khaki trousers, he lets his guard down. He wants to know more about the previous owner. He opens the door and lets the monsters in. Then there are faces and memories. No images of the owner, but of their family and friends. What they could see. Rudy recognizes a kitchen that he has been in, the same house he found these pants.

There is a woman there, her back to him. She is cooking at the stove. The kitchen smells like onions fried in butter. Two blurs go past his vision. A child chasing another child.

There is a second set of images. A different woman resting on a couch. She is buried under heavy blankets. She tries to force a smile as a hand in the foreground gives her a fresh cup of tea with honey melted into it.

Rudy sees the shoes in the vision. He is wearing those same too loose Italian shoes.

There are five more, seven in total. Each from a different house. Each one Rudy remembers. The various articles of clothing on him start to itch.

He realizes that all the items he is wearing are commandeered from different residences. The jacket, his shirt, his pants, his belt, his underwear, his socks and his shoes each have different origins. He has not been paying close attention. They wear out at different rates. The planets circle the sun at different intervals but eventually they line up.

The images become concurrent instead of sequential. Rudy feels himself submerged, and tries hard to hang onto control. To hang onto his memories, his own name.

His limbs begin to rebel. Too many people fighting over the steering wheel as the bus begins to swerve. He thinks *I need to remove some of these items. I have passed some critical mass. I have acquired too many opponents, too many occupiers.*

He tries first to remove the coat, but his body does not cooperate. His legs thrust out in different directions. He is too confused to make a sound.

Overhead, the crows take notice. They begin to call out. No imitation sounds, no cat sounds or raven sounds or machine sounds. Just alarms. They all say the same thing but not in sync.

The Italian shoes clink together like beer steins, and Rudy loses his balance. He spins a quarter turn and falls backward away from the street and into a blackberry bush.

His landing disrupts the local ecology. Juncos and chickadees take to the air, abandoning a safe shelter. They fly low to avoid the attention of birds of prey.

A single field mouse bolts from his space where he has lived protected by the thorns. He heads directly to another bush only twenty feet away.

Rudy has landed on his back, knees up high. The vines and thorns have absorbed his impact and bounced back up. The thorns have grabbed him in numerous places. He struggles to get free, to get back to his feet. His jacket is thoroughly snagged as are the lower sections of his pants.

He tries to roll out of the bush, but it twists with him. The images of wives and children in rooms and backyards continue to flash into his mind.

He opens his mouth to yell for help, but his voice is not there and none of his passengers are near the microphone. The spirits pile on top of him, holding him down, pushing his consciousness down. He is not afraid of falling asleep and losing consciousness. He is afraid of losing his persona, his psyche.

He thinks he hears snorting and growling. *I know who I am.* His limbs pulling in different directions. A self-imposed drawing and quartering. The forces cancel out, and he stays spiked and speared on a mattress of thorns. Seven is at least two too many. No voices, just images. They weigh on him, holding him down. His essence is deluded amongst seven others.

Rudy searches his memory for something old, an anchor, but finds nothing to save him. His eyes close and now he sees familiar faces. Three women he does know, superimposed over each other. They alternate, a rotation between three channels.

The fortune teller turns into the redheaded girl turns into Freya. They each look concerned, but they just watch.

Harvey and Roscoe and Gideon are further back, over the shoulders of the women.

The crows fly lower, their wings brush against him, trying to to stir him.

He wriggles in his trap. The tentacles of the blackberries and the teeth of the blackberries hold him without any fatigue.

Rudy hears the crows. *I know all their voices and they are all distinct and separate to me.* Even Grendel's voice as it pretends or imitates the others gives away his identity.

A bird lands on his chest. He feels its feet repositioning with energy, but no plan. He opens his eyes to see Grendel on his stomach.

The other five are in the background, flying in wild patterns, filling the air with sound and feathers. It looks like a hundred crows. It sounds like a hundred crows.

Grendel makes eye contact and holds a stare.

Rudy cannot say anything, but he thinks *yes I still know you. I am still Rudy Lafferty.*

Grendel makes a sound no crow should make. It is not melodic. It does not contain information or meaning or memory. It is a sound of a mimicry machine left for years in a factory full of unmaintained heavy equipment.

It is metal on metal. It is a belt that is slipping, a motor out of time. It is a complicated pattern that will take hours to repeat as all the frequencies align again.

But Grendel does not have that much wind. The noise lasts fourteen seconds. The noise stuns all the occupants of Rudy's body. It is enough for him to think coherently for a few seconds.

He slides one arm, and then the other out of his jacket.

He reaches down and undoes his belt. He slides it out of its loops and flings it over his head further from the road.

He leans forward enough to slide his shoes off even while they are still tied. They are loose enough to allow this to work.

He pushes himself up and away from the bush,

even though its thorns dig into the palms of his hands. Blood and meat for the blackberries.

As he regains his feet, he bends down and removes both socks. He tosses them deep into the blackberry bush. An offering to appease monsters. The socks will end up as useful, though unorthodox, nesting material for two different animals.

Rudy takes inventory. He is down to only three pieces of clothing: a shirt, the pants, his underwear. He has no trouble now assuming control of his body.

His pant legs show numerous snags from the blackberries. He is only bleeding from his hands.

He turns to face the blackberry bush. He does not want to turn his back on his attacker.

His jacket is thoroughly tangled in the vines and thorns. Though it will not be digested, it is fully trapped. It will not be dislodged in one piece. It has become part of the structure of the bush. A roof or a canopy for small creatures to hide under. As the bush continues to grow, the jacket will be buried further below. A fossil from another time. An older layer of strata.

The crows are quiet now. Rudy spots them in nearby trees.

Seven is at least two too many. He will plan more carefully the composition of his wardrobe. *I need shoes so I'll have to try these back on.*

He puts first the left shoe on and waits for the arrival of the spirits. Nothing happens so he adds the other. His shoes are even more sloppy on his feet now with no socks.

If I choose pants carefully, I can do without a belt. Socks are the cheapest thing. I can use a little money to buy some pairs. Socks that have not been previously owned. Socks without history. Socks without residents.

He thinks *if I have more items from the same home, same previous owner, there will be less of them to gang up on me. I can get some things from my current place. I really need new pants. I definitely need a new jacket.*

Rudy walks back to his current temporary residence. He removes every article clothing and puts them all in the garbage can. He scrubs himself red in the shower.

Like a mantra, he repeats with water rushing into his mouth. "I am Rudy Lafferty. I was a butcher. This body belongs to me and only me."

The juncos and chickadees return to their nests. They inspect and accept the jacket. The field mouse prefers his new den.

53 - More Accurately Wyverns

With no adherence to workdays or weekends, double-crested cormorants swim in Commencement Bay searching for fish. *Nannopterum auritum.*

Underwater, they become spear guns. Their demonstration of velocity and accuracy unwitnessed by surface dwellers.

When the sun reaches its midday apex, they perch on top of one of the wood pilings protruding in the shallow water along Ruston Way. If there is no sun that day, the cormorants follow the script regardless. If you follow Ruston Way along the water, you will end up at Point Defiance Park. The cormorants do not travel there.

They present their wings to dry their feathers and warm their bones. Their snaky heads look more reptilian than avian.

Their dark silhouettes remember tiny dragons,

concocted of obsidian and pitch. Or more accurately, wyverns with two wings and only two legs.

They pose like fashion models. They pose like bodybuilders.

The play continues on to a third act which sees the birds taking positions on the hawsers that connect the *S.S. Cape Island* and *S.S. Cape Intrepid* to the dock. These two monotone gray ships seem more like buildings made entirely of right angles. They travel from their moorings almost as often as buildings do. Most Tacomans have never spotted human activity on the boats. They are ghost ships commandeered by the birds.

The cormorants space themselves about five feet apart on the lines. Equidistant like Christmas lights on a string if all the lights were black. They have experience in social distancing since the day of dinosaurs.

They are plague ready. They are plague-proof. They are waiting out the empire. Cormorants have outlived many kingdoms.

One of the birds extends a wing to shake out an itch. His neighbor leans away, but does not move his feet.

54 – Eggs Every Morning

"Good morning neighbor."

Rudy's right hand goes back to the doorknob on the front porch. His knees bend and prepare to spring into a run.

A man crosses the subtle boundary between the front yards of the two houses. Rudy thinks the man is of Japanese ancestry. His age is difficult to estimate. His face is gaunt but with very few wrinkles. His hair is more gray than white.

The neighbor realizes Rudy is not going to answer. He says, "Please do not worry. I know that you are not the new owner. You are the new resident. I knew the family. There was a death. They did not want to stay here anymore. I watched them drive away."

He extends his hand. "My name is Jushiro but you can call me what my students used to call me. They called me Mr. Joshua."

Later they are sitting on a cast-iron bench in front of Mr. Joshua's house. He has brought out two cups of oolong tea.

Mr. Joshua says, "You may notice this wedding ring is now the wrong size. The Band-Aid keeps it from running off and rolling away. This used to fit snug before my wife passed away. She used to make me eggs every morning even when we both worked. Also elaborate lunches. I was envied by my fellow teachers. If she was mad at me, she would send me with far too much food. To make me think about her longer. Think about what I did wrong. I now make eggs for myself every morning, and they are awful. It appears that I am too old to learn this. Or it could be to master this would minimize her. She was such a good cook. Now I go through a lot of Band-Aids."

He points at Rudy's left hand. "Has there ever been a ring on that finger?"

Rudy thinks. Rudy pauses. Rudy opens his mouth to answer but closes it without a word.

"Look at me asking funny questions. A reasonable response would be yes or no, but I sense you wanted to say something like I don't know or I don't remember and those are not reasonable answers."

Rudy and Mr. Joshua are eating dinner inside Mr. Joshua's house. The portions are small, and the meat is overcooked. Rudy eats his vegetables, but Mr. Joshua does not.

Mr. Joshua says, "I was told by my father that if you see yourself walking around, if you see your doppelgänger, then you are soon to die."

Rudy asks, "Did you see your doppelgänger?"

"No, but she did. That is to say, she saw hers."

Neither of them says a word for more than a full minute.

Mr. Joshua says, "I have a theory that my wife and I both live in a world where the other has passed. The world is curious to taste all possible pains, so it chooses both. It is an unnecessary cruelty. Undoubtedly, she is doing better than me. She was smaller than I am. This shirt was hers and now it is too big for me."

Mr. Joshua clears the dinner plates. He says, "My life has fewer people in it now. Just a few survivors of a war, but there has been no war. My life is a vampire movie without a vampire. Just a shrinking cast."

He folds his hands in front of him. "I have looked for the villains in my life. Someone to be angry with. I have found only moments of cowardice, follies of miscommunication, and the influence of ghosts."

Rudy and Mr. Joshua are sitting on the bench again two days later.

Mr. Joshua says, "I have been writing a book. I have written others. Published most of them. But this is the most important one. This one is about her. In the book, she is alone in this same house after I have died. Every day I write a chapter detailing what she does that day. It is mundane and tedious and boring, and I'm extremely proud of it. There is no war. There are no vampires. The book is full of her days spent gardening and cooking meals for one. Simple things like renewing a driver's license or struggling to fall asleep. She was always a bad sleeper. I don't think that would have got any better without me."

"I am afraid that if I stop writing the book that she will truly be gone. You want to know how long I've been working on this book. For nearly two and a half years. I assume you can do the math. I used to teach math. I have almost nine hundred chapters written all in long hand. The book has become a monster. It is taken over two full rooms in my house. No one has read any of it and you will not read any of it either. I am getting very tired, but I cannot stop. I wonder if she is doing the same for me. She was a painter, not a writer. I write my chapters in the morning before the sun comes up. I know what will happen in her day before I know much about mine. In every chapter she takes time to paint."

55 – The Song of Bowie

Bowie struggles to keep up with the other five.

While they can afford to be flamboyant, carving elaborate shapes in the air, he becomes very linear and pragmatic.

He is slowing, which makes him vulnerable to cats and birds of prey. His mate notices the change and brings him extra food. She blocks the wind at night. She is not slowing down.

The group travels long distances to accompany the man. They pass through the territory of one large group of crows, and then another. They are asked for explanations, but they have no explanations.

Bowie is worried about the wild one. The one that should not be here. The one who cheats the wind when he flies with his broken wing. He has grown too reckless. He gets too close to people. He lands on their shoulders. He tempts cats to leap at him. He is louder and stronger than all of the others.

Bowie does not understand how he knows, but he knows this is the day.

He is without hunger, though his mouth is very dry. Too dry for water to do any good.

He selects a moment when he is lagging behind. When he is not in view of the others.

He darts off in a different direction in silence. He keeps low to the ground, choosing shadowy places.

Bowie is not looking for a specific place. The place will choose him.

He lands on a raised flower bed. Three varieties of pansies in a geometric pattern.

He knows they will find him by making larger and larger concentric circles. They will be loud and each will behave in a different manner when they find him.

It is so warm in the sun that he shivers.

He has no voice left and he brings in his wings to his body.

He listens for what the end sounds like. It sounds exactly like he thought it would. It is a song full of noise and silence.

56 – The Maze

To keep running, to cycle through all the houses. A century could be spent this way. The trajectory evolves from a line into something two dimensional, something not unlike a street map of Tacoma.

Rudy sits on the ground and closes his eyes. He stops thinking about running. Stops thinking about just surviving and just avoiding his fate.

Where does this body want to go?

He is not sleeping. He is not daydreaming. He is seeking navigation.

Go to the water. Go west and go north. Return to water.

He opens his eyes and finds his sitting body has rotated slightly. He is pointed in a different direction. He believes this direction is roughly northwest.

He stands, and he starts to walk. There are backyards in the way. He resists the urge to hop fences.

His feet are not loyal and true. His path resembles that of a dancer crossing a ballroom when the song has another verse left.

His pockets are empty.

He is guided by the sun. He does not know if the moon is watching him and reporting on his movements.

His corvid entourage follows him but stays out of his view. They do not announce their pursuit. There are only five. Rudy has not been paying attention to them. He has not noticed their diminished number.

Rudy passes people on the sidewalk. People pushing strollers, people walking dogs, people holding hands. He does not acknowledge any of them.

He comes to a green space, a community garden. Vegetables and flowers. Twenty different ways to use the soil.

Five crows land in front of him barring his way forward. They oppose each other in silence.

He owes them an explanation, an answer, but he is not sure he has one. He thinks it is disrespectful to stand above them. He sits down in the garden and begins to speak without knowing what he will say.

"I've been running too long. It has been two and a half years I think but it feels like a hundred. The city has emptied out. I have not been able to hang on to anyone. I miss the ones I shared a room with or shared a roof with. I don't know if they are still here. If they are still alive or if they are dead. I'm afraid to find out. I have walked and run until I am just muscle and tendons and bones."

He pauses and counts. "Why are there only five of you? Where is Bowie?"

The crows do not react. They are solemn listeners.

"Will I lose each of you? One at a time. You've protected me, saved me more than once."

There are pedestrians passing alongside the garden. They do not stop to observe the gathering. A man speaking to a murder of attentive crows is not necessarily a crazy person, but it is wise to give him plenty of room.

Rudy stops talking, and then time passes. Who knows how much time? Thirty minutes, an hour, two and a half years.

He resumes his quest with the crows now forming their typical around him as he continues to head north and west. They are heading toward Point Defiance Park.

The park contains the Point Defiance Zoo and Aquarium, Fort Nisqually, multiple gardens, a pagoda, tennis courts, and more. There is a pond at the entrance where Canada geese rule and ducks are tolerated.

Black-tailed deer sleep in the park at night. *Odocoileus hemionus columbianus.*

Much of the park is forest crisscrossed by brachial walking trails. On a map they look like the spikes of a single wheel. On the ground, their fractal complexity is revealed. Bring water. Bring a compass.

The park is encircled by the paved Five Mile Drive, much of it now closed due to ongoing erosion.

The forest is between Rudy and the water. The trails do not align with his overall direction. He compromises to go a little to the right with the intent of correcting at the next junction, but the maze does not give him that option.

The tree canopy is dense, and he cannot rely on the sun for direction. He becomes lost and disoriented. Dehydrated. The crows are his halo, but not his scouts.

Each tree looks familiar, those that are upright and those that have fallen. He thinks he is repeating steps, making loops, stacking his footprints.

He comes to an open clearing. He has not seen another walker or a hiker for several minutes. The forest eats all sound. He sits on the ground. He rolls over onto his side and closes his eyes.

Just for a moment just for a minute just for a second.

57 – Crow Funeral

A crow funeral does not require an invitation. Think of it as a broadcast announcement at a certain frequency. Bouncing on the ether. Heard miles and miles away. If you can hear it and you can understand it, consider yourself invited.

The skies blacken. The sun in midday form has thrown a black cloak over its face and turned away for a few heartbeats.

There is noise and there is commotion. Crows do not go anywhere quietly and certainly not when in great numbers.

It is the wrong time of the day. They normally make their journeys in the morning when the sun comes up and in the evening near dusk.

They make a noisy blanket in the sky, passing over roads and houses. Drivers roll down their windows to hear them and to take in the scope of the congregation.

As the crows arrive near where Rudy has lain down, people are chased out of the park. There is no official evacuation, but visitors draw the same conclusion.

It looks like a horror movie. It looks like the end of the world. It is an airborne amphitheater that is circling.

The man is a curiosity. He has been an odd bird walking through the city. The six crows, now five, have followed him through unfamiliar neighborhoods. They have made peace with other groups of crows. They are pilgrims.

These crows in close proximity to each other share their unique and distinct songs. The songs they have invented, the songs they have stolen.

For several hours, no crows were seen on Sixth Avenue. No crows were seen in the Proctor District. And so on.

Five crows form a perimeter around the body on the ground. New arrivals descend to test him with their beaks, to see if he is still alive. Then one of the five will chase the newcomer away.

When the end comes, there is a sound. It is not a trumpet. This is no Book of Revelations type of thing. It is too loud to be coming from a bird that could ride on your shoulder.

The sound comes from Grendel.

It does not resemble anything organic or natural. It feels like the grinding of gears under the earth. Gears that are slowed down by the resistance of many feet of soil.

It sounds like the end of a basketball game but acts as more of an all-clear signal.

The crows begin to leave after that. Not as a single group. Not in a single direction. They shake off the spell and return to their own territories. Their expanse and their multitude for a time is exposed to all.

The people of Tacoma connect the two events. The end of the lockdown when normalcy attempts to return to the city and to the world. That same day, the crows flew to Point Defiance Park creating a near eclipse, possibly apocalyptic or biblical.

Someone asks how many crows there were. The wisest person within earshot says, "All of the crows."

58 - Sleeper

The woman who first told Rudy that he would die walks into the clearing near where his body rests.

She is wearing a brown leather jacket over a long yellow sundress and hiking boots. Her right hand holds something under the jacket close to her body.

She notices only Rudy and takes two small steps towards him.

Lazarus drops from a nearby branch to come between her and the sleeper. She takes two stumbling steps backwards before she lands on her tailbone. She can feel the mud on her legs and seeping through her dress.

Something has been dropped and rolls a few feet in front of her.

A dagger with a well-maintained blade and a topaz embedded in the hilt. The fortune teller crawls toward the blade.

Grendel is there first and tries to lift it. It is too heavy, and he can only flip it over.

Other black shapes appear. There are five crows between her and the weapon.

She leans back in the mud with her hands in front of her face. A request for truce and also protection from attack.

She looks at Rudy and sees no indication of life. No signs of breathing. The complaints from the crows have not been heard by him.

She wants to poke him. To feel his wrist. To put a mirror under his mouth and nose. Some way to know if he is alive. She cannot leave without knowing but the way to confirm this is blocked.

She waits. She is very accomplished at waiting.

Her jacket pockets are purposefully empty. There is no food to offer the crows. No identification. Nothing useful.

Ten minutes pass.

All five crows rise off the ground and find low perches near Rudy.

She has heard nothing to startle the crows. She scans the perimeter of the clearing.

From the same direction that she has come, a figure enters. From her sitting vantage point, she estimates it is more than seven feet tall. Earth toned clothing, green and brown. No sound from its feet stepping through the gravel and leaves and twigs.

She is not sure those are feet. They are just solid shapes at the end of the legs without toes or laces or other features.

The figure takes no notice of her. It passes inches away from her without making contact.

She looks up to the face to identify it, to

understand it. She wants to ask it many questions.

What she sees stifles those questions. The face is not human and maybe not even a face at all. She notices its eyes and mouth seem like the accidental byproducts of overlays of leaves and branches and sheets of tree bark.

The figure lowers in front of Rudy. It slides its arms under his body. It scoops him up like a forklift.

She hears creaks like wood under pressure. Under stress and strain. The process of getting back to its previous posture is slow. She sees one of the feet slip in the wet leaves but regain its footing.

The crows are silent during all of this. They are all turned towards the figure, but do not interfere. They are entranced.

With Rudy high up against its chest, the figure strides away from the clearing. It makes its way opposite from the direction it had arrived. It does not follow the man-made paths. It finds openings between trees. Steps over fallen logs. It lands softly and makes minor adjustments to its shape to fit into narrow spaces. It moves at a steady escalator-type pace.

The fortune teller moves towards the dagger and grabs it before the crows notice. She runs after the figure.

The figure does not leave any wake in its passing. It travels cleanly through the woods. A well-executed cut.

It does leave prints in the damp ground. These prints will puzzle hikers tomorrow who cannot identify them as animal tracks or as shoe prints. One man will decide it must have been some sort of machine. Some equipment deployed by the people who work at the park.

The fortune teller does not always fit in the space the figure has traveled through. When she chooses another way, she gets a face full of spiderwebs.

She holds the dagger out in front of her. This is a borrowed thing that she does not know how to wield. Part of her wants to attack the thing. To stab it and stop it from taking Rudy away. She does not know if she should try to stop it.

She had not quite formulated a plan for some stealth stabbing with the dagger. The reason she came here. She could not visualize how that would actually go. She resigned herself to improvise. She would figure it out in the moment. But using the dagger as a weapon against the striding figure is not something she wants to try.

She runs while it walks. She steps into a hole and twists her ankle. She leans up against a fallen log, a tree felled by a lightning strike. She rubs her ankle and determines the injury is minor.

The log is softer than she expected. She finds the wood is covered with multiple types of fungus. Shades of green and gray and white. She thinks of the inhabitants of coral reefs moving with the current.

Then she notices the motion of ants as they rush over the surface of the log toward her from all directions. She pushes off from the dead tree and sweeps her jacket and dress free of any insects.

As she resumes following the figure, her skin itches. She assumes she is carrying some tiny passengers.

The strider and the pursuer cross the road in the park twice. She can see no variation from a perfectly straight line. She thinks they are heading due west.

The trajectory ends at a cliff facing the water. Off to the left, she can see the twin Tacoma Narrows Bridges that connect Tacoma to the Kitsap Peninsula.

The figure stops at the top of the cliff for a moment. There is an adjustment, a shift of weight, a recalibration of vertebrae and knees. Then the shape starts walking down the cliff face.

She reaches the cliff top but cannot follow. The descent is nearly vertical. She watches the progress of the figure down the hillside. The movement is not perfect. She can see tiny rockslides as its footing slips briefly before stabilizing. She loses track of it as the trees obscure her line of sight.

She anticipates where it will emerge by the waterline. She counts the beats in her head. Her estimates of time and location are very accurate. The figure reappears and continues to walk directly into the water. Without slowing down. Without adjusting its cargo.

Then it is gone, and Rudy is gone with it.

She waits for something to rise in the water. Some disturbance on the surface, but nothing is visible. She imagines that this thing might walk along the bottom of the Narrows and arrive on the other side. She would not be able to see that from her location. She chooses to believe that both of them are claimed by the water and swept away by the current.

There is nothing else to be done. Her errand is both unfinished and irrelevant. Her weapon to be returned from where it was borrowed. Her clothes are to be washed. She is sure there are some ants crawling on her legs. She will not be at peace until she sees them rinsed down a shower drain.

She does not follow her same path back. She follows Five Mile Drive out of the park. She avoids ants and spiderwebs. She avoids a second confrontation with the murder of crows.

59 – Chained to a Missile

Three nights before the man in the brown uniform will come to take away the oxygen tank and to not leave a new tank, there is a knock at Freya's apartment door.

Three days before Rudy will walk toward Point Defiance Park.

She looks at the clock. 3:15 AM. She has been in and out of sleep. Deep in fever. Sweating, and a bit confused.

She ignores the knocking. It stops.

Then the knocking transforms into a pounding, which lasts only a few seconds.

Freya gets to her feet and stares at the door.

She hears a hand on the doorknob and an effort to turn it.

She is awake now. Her head cleared.

She walks into the kitchen with soft steps. She searches for anything to protect herself.

She maneuvers an old frying pan out of the cupboard without it clanging against other metal objects. There is a dent on this pan from previous necessary activity. This frying pan works on skulls.

She takes a steak knife from the silverware drawer. The blade has not been sharpened during the time she has owned it. This knife will barely cut through baked chicken, and it is useless on actual steak. She hopes her attacker tends towards poultry in its protective skin.

She approaches the door with the frying pan in her left hand and the knife in her right. She realizes that she has this backward. Right hand is for strength and the left hand for precision. She switches the objects in her hands.

She thinks now would be a good time to still have that sword.

The noises at the door stop. She does not hear anyone walk away. She is too smart to take the bait. She does not open the door

She lowers herself down to the carpet. She puts her makeshift weapons down beside her.

On the night before the man in the brown uniform will come to take away the oxygen tank and to not leave a new tank, Freya takes mouse steps towards the bathroom to see herself in the mirror that she has not cleaned in months. She sees her hollow face and her sunken eyes.

Those light blue eyes designed for those who hunt near the arctic circle. The ones that ask a tithe to share the territory. Fenris spawn.

Her gray t-shirt and equally gray sweatpants are heavy with her. She has been boiled and wilted. Ten percent of her body weight has been converted into sweat and phlegm. Her clothes have absorbed and held onto an insulating layer of brine.

Two of the three lights in the bathroom are burned out. She needs to get new lightbulbs, but probably not today.

She notices her hair has gone white. She says, "This is a year to remember, but I probably won't."

She does remember last night when she had started saying things not in her own voice. By the time she had looped back around to repeat what she had said moments before, she had grabbed a notebook. As she put the words to paper, starting from the middle of the second pass until the middle of the third pass, the unfamiliar voice left her.

Today she finds that piece of paper wadded up in the trashcan. She unfolds it and tries to read her own writing. It talks about the arctic fox, and other tundra creatures that change and grow white hair as fall turns into winter. To become invisible in the snow. Then it turns into the field notes of someone else and the language changes. She thinks it is French, but she does not speak French. She surely does not write French, so the words are phonetically spelled out.

She walks back toward her bedroom. She does not trust her reduced weight to stay safely above her feet. She does not trust her ankles to guide her toes to true and safe landings on the thin carpet.

She wraps her arms around the oxygen tank and kisses its crown. She says, "You rat bastard, you motherfucker, you will not be missed."

She has been chained to a missile for too long.

Freya does not sleep that night. She needs time away from that bed which has not been kind to her elbows and her hips and her knees.

The man who comes to the door is younger than her. He is not wearing a mask. She is not wearing a mask.

She has the equipment in two boxes which she sets next to his hand truck.

She says, "I could eat an entire pizza right now, maybe two."

The young man develops a stutter for the first time in his life. He thinks this is the wrong time for it to arrive.

While he struggles to answer, she fills the space. "I am just offering you a pizza. Just a pizza. If you are not hungry, I am fully capable of eating a whole one myself."

He looks again at his work order printout to find her name. He tells her his name. He thinks he got that right. Pretty sure.

"I will clean up first," she says. "These…" she grabs her t-shirt up near her collarbone. "These are not gonna ever be clean again. Washing will be a waste of time and water. I would like to burn them. Can you help with that too?"

Freya does not talk much over dinner. She chews on a slice while her hand is ready to reload with another slice.

His stutter is gone by the time the second pizza is brought to the table. He is actually hungry and splits it with Freya. This is also an intervention. So that she does not explode as a dog might do if given an unlimited pile of food.

He has rescued her from a desert island or a makeshift raft at sea.

She looks at him as she eats, and as he talks. She smiles between bites showing canines that have never been realigned by braces.

She stares at his ears, and he hears her laugh for the first time.

60 – The Spaceship Expels Its Passengers

For two and a half years, the B-movie spaceship mislabeled as Saint Joseph Medical Center has been out of balance. It has been taking on new passengers, either those walking in or carried in or wheeled in. The flow of passengers leaving the ship had been pinched and throttled down. The state rooms must now be filled to capacity. So many eyes at those porthole windows on all nine floors.

Today, the river reverses and corrects. There are more departures than admissions. More landing parties are dispatched to various parts of Tacoma.

Anastasia stomps out the front door, which almost makes the mistake of not opening in time. Her hair has grown down to her shoulders. A wide brush stroke of straight light brown hair at her roots chases the from-a-bottle red curls at the end.

Her black tights are crooked and torn but they help against the cold. She came in on a warmer day so she has no jacket. Now she walks fast to keep warm.

She paces at a bus stop at the top of the hill. She has only twenty minutes of patience today during which exactly no buses arrive. This is in direct conflict with a timetable posted on the bus shelter. She might have the day wrong.

She puts her left hand out in front of her and lets it wobble like a divining rod. Her hand selects the direction as the crow flies, which is diagonal to the grid of streets.

Her boots hit the pavement hard, and the impact hurts the sidewalk.

Two young men turn to the approaching noise, expecting to see a herd of large men. They shuffle across the street to get out of her way.

Anastasia had torn up her name tag on the day she was admitted to the hospital months ago. Just before she was discharged, she was still destroying tags or any of the documents bearing her name.

She has completely lost her fetish for all things medical. She is tired of everyone around her knowing her name and everything about her. They called her by that name, which didn't seem familiar to her. There are no secrets in a hospital bed. It is a gross realm of bodily fluids and frozen clocks.

One nurse chose to place her ungloved hand on Anastasia's brow that first day. She pulled it back in alarm.

"You are burning up."

Anastasia had replied, "I know. I've been telling people for years. I am volcanic."

She learns to hate thermometers and needles

and pills and those ugly hospital gowns. It takes months to stop being a radiating body of pure heat. For the crazy words to stop filling her mouth. Once in middle of the night, she had spoken steadily for more than five minutes, in what she assumed was Russian.

Three days ago, she had woken up in her hospital bed. A woman she had never seen before was standing next to the bed.

Her room was poorly lit. It was well past visiting hours. The woman did not introduce herself.

She had said, "I am looking for someone. Someone who stayed with you. His name is Rudy Lafferty. It is very important that I find him."

Anastasia had wiped her left hand across her eyes. Trying to wake up, trying to assess the situation.

"I don't know anyone by that name."

The stranger had said, "Listen, Anastasia…"

"Wait. You don't get to use my name. You don't get to say it out loud unless you tell me yours," Anastasia had interrupted.

The stranger smiled. Shiny white teeth stand out on a tanned face. "Okay. No names. I have a picture of this Rudy. Let me show you on my phone."

In the picture, Rudy is behind a counter wearing a white apron. He is not smiling, and he is not posing for the camera.

"Oh, the butcher. Yes, but I last saw him months ago. He left suddenly. Something happened. He got scared and never came back."

The stranger had taken back her phone. Anastasia had continued to focus on the woman's face. She did not want to lose her in the darkness. She felt like she was negotiating with a cobra.

"He is good at running. So, you've not seen him since? Are you sure?"

"Yes. When he left, I got sick. Then I ended up here."

The stranger had responded, "I see. I'm sorry that you got sick. That should never have happened. All of this could have been prevented. I had the chance at the beginning to stop it, but I didn't understand then. I found his trail a few times, even though I was not looking. I was... notified when he visited my old place."

The stranger had turned away, and Anastasia could not see her teeth anymore. The stranger had run her hand through her long hair.

"But I know you are getting better. In fact, I could see you walking out of here in a few days."

The stranger left then. Anastasia had listened closely for the sound of fading footsteps but heard nothing.

Anastasia had decided at that moment that she wanted to be out of the hospital before that woman visited again. She had no way to warn Rudy.

Today, she compensates for the diagonal nature of her path by alternating directions to cross streets. She does not wait for crosswalk signs to give permission. She gives the death glare to drivers to get them to yield.

She has a job to do. A quarter of the wind's directions have been unguarded for months. Has she been replaced? Have her housemates compensated and spread their territory to accommodate?

The other residents of the house could not have found her or tracked her down. They do not know her name to ask for at a hospital front desk. They would not be able to recognize her name in an obituary column. Too many names in those columns anyway.

When she arrives home, her housemates are glad to see her. They had watched her fight the illness. They had insisted that she get medical help.

They all look older. The man with the goatee tries to hide fact he is crying. The muscular woman approaches for a hug but switches to a fist bump. The man who writes screenplays puts his hand to his chest and sighs.

She goes to her room without saying a word. She turns the music up loud and gets into fresh warmer clothes.

61 - Monday

The next Monday feels like the very first Monday.

People see people they have not seen in two and a half years. Some are too familiar and desperate when they grip their co-workers. Others will not shake hands.

Some forgot how far apart to stand. How loud to talk. How to make eye contact.

Some people do not look like their passport photo, not like their driver's license. Some nearly starved. Some ate like every day was the very last day.

Some did not remember until Tuesday that Monday means shoes and bras and real pants and combed hair and showers.

Companies struggle to get their offices ready for workers again. The roads are overwhelmed.

Death tracker websites shut down.

An Irish pub in the Stadium District runs out of Jameson whiskey and Guinness. The customers do not leave. A man writes two names on the chalkboard above the urinal trough in the men's room. Two people he cannot find. Two people he is worried about.

Danny Winfield walks from the bus stop towards St. Joe's emergency room. There are several crows nearby and he gives them their room. He never turns his back on crows. He digs in his pocket and tosses some dog treats on the ground, far away from his walking path. An offering, an appeasement, a truce.

Danny instinctively puts his hands to his face when the crows approach. The scratches on his cheek are scarred over now. He remembers the feel of their claws on his face.

He cannot tell crows apart. He thinks the group that follows him is the same group that attacked him. But these are opportunist crows who have snagged him in this routine.

Zee fared far better than Danny. She has one small white spot along her jaw line. She has become skilled at covering it with a small amount of cream on workdays or days that she plans to go out. Her reactions were quicker as her hands were not occupied by restraining Rudy. She protected her face with one hand and threw a fist wildly with the other.

She does not feed crows. She yells at them on the street. She is working the same shift as Danny. This is one of the things they will not talk about.

Harvey Burgess is on a plane to Nairobi, Kenya. He wonders about the scars on his cheeks which he has had all his life. They are flaring up, red and tender. Something is going to happen.

He enjoyed his time in Nairobi. Next year was a good year. He hopes last year will be a good one too.

62 – Empty Handed

A man gets on his flight at Shanghai Pudong International Airport with no luggage and no carry-on bag and no phone and no wallet and no money and no toothbrush. He is a zero.

In his pocket, he has forged documents and a bus pass to get him from SeaTac Airport back to Tacoma.

These objects are not helpful in getting food or drink or even clean clothes.

Unlike most of the Americans who pass through this airport, he can read the Chinese characters on the signs.

Gideon has been gone for almost two years. He has dropped weight, and his head has been shaved. He has spent too much time in the sun unprotected. A desert creature entering the city.

His clothes, not his clothes, hang loosely on his

tall frame. These had belonged to a man who had died a few feet away from him. They were better than the ones Gideon was wearing, so like a hermit crab, he traded up.

He is missing the pinky finger on his left hand. He will never tell anyone how this happened. He is willing to throw fists to avoid telling. His luck was just good enough that day to see this day.

He has doused himself in samples from the duty-free cologne gauntlet in the airport to cover up his odor.

He relaxes as he enters the plane. He had been trapped in a small room for thirty minutes as a man asked him repeatedly the same questions about his identity. He was told his face did not match the white face in his photo. That he did not match the western name on his paperwork that Gideon had memorized until it felt authentic.

The man would only speak to him in Mandarin. Accused him of being a local trying to pass himself off as something else.

In the end, his interrogator had told him to enjoy America but find a better forger next time. It was disrespectful to bring something so unprofessional into this room.

Gideon had not come to China through an airport. A man with a wet cough and a fever was not allowed on any airplane.

He had traveled across the Pacific in the hold of a ship. Quarantined from the crew with enough food and water if he planned well.

Upon arrival, he was cured but changed. Unrecognizable to the people who had locked him down below. They inspected the hold, expecting to find a dead American or at least the shed skin of what they had brought onboard.

Then a shorter voyage, relying on false papers into Shanghai. There he found a place he could not have prepared for. He had brought enough money for a few months, maybe six.

The flight attendant puts a tray of food in front of him. He eats without pause and without judgement. His mind does not slow down enough to process the flavor or quality or even the food group of what he is eating. The elderly woman next to him gives him the items on her tray that she does not want.

While walking through the airport, he had added to his possessions. He had grabbed a pen from an airline's customer service counter.

He had picked up several discarded flyers written in Mandarin from the tile floor. He had noticed the backs of the flyers were blank.

On the plane, he writes in small print on the back of the flyers, trying to optimize the space. He oscillates between his native English and the more complicated Chinese characters. He does not realize he is doing this.

This is the beginning of a book. He has already written this out in full once.

The book is a search for a person who remains unnamed and unfound in its pages. It is both surreal and unrealistic. It is entirely true.

Someone who he had thought of as a friend had tossed the manuscript onto the fire. This happened on a day that was too hot to require any heat from that fire.

If the pages had been fed one by one in sequence into the flames, Gideon could have read them aloud. Then at least two of them would know all the words.

He can rewrite the book without omission, because it is all in his feet and it is in his hands. The book is recorded in his bones.

He runs out of blank space just before the pen runs out of ink. There are still many pages left to write.

He folds the pieces of paper like elegant napkins and places them in his pockets.

He checks and sees that there are still nine hours of flight time before arrival.

With the complementary headphones, he watches Chinese films with English subtitles and then he watches American films with Chinese subtitles. He is trying to reteach his brain to identify and understand his native language.

He will not return to China. He did not find what he was looking for. He found no resolution no death notice no grave no eyewitness' account at the end of someone's life. No trail to follow and no reunion. Too many people lost and so many missing. Who could find a single specific person in plague times?

There was a man who gave him the vegetables too poor to be served in his restaurant along with watered down broth. He told Gideon that this is not the true city. The world is broken, and this is a substitute. Do not judge this place based on the face of the imposter he has seen. The real city will return when the plague has gone. When it is safe again.

Gideon had told him it was same for his city.

When he finally conceded defeat, when he knew he would never find the man he was searching for, when he had access to a phone, he called his parents.

He had asked for money for airfare and for forged papers. They sent him just enough money and a bus pass.

He moves through SeaTac Airport without incident.

The Sound Transit bus drops him off at the station near the Tacoma Dome where he will transfer to another bus.

His parents will arrive at his place in two days. They are driving their motor home up from California.

There will be lectures on reckless behavior and responsibility. They will want to know everything. There is so little he can actually tell them. They will not understand it. They would not believe most of it.

His priority is to keep the pages in his pocket dry. They crinkle as he boards the bus that will drop him off a few blocks from his house. He hopes Rudy has taken good care of his place while he has been gone.

The first thing he notices in Tacoma is the number of birds. He counts at least seven different species on his walk home from the bus stop.

Someone had told him that Shanghai translated to "no birds anymore."

Everywhere in Tacoma he sees crows.

Acknowledgements

I would like to thank the first readers who traveled through the writing of this book with me: Kris Becker, Scott Russell. It is a better book for their care and feedback.

In honor of the kind people who passed away recently and too soon: Danny Orbeck, Maurice Stewart, Sam Tiam, Noel Webster, Chandler O'Leary.

This is a work of fiction that takes place in a fictionalized version of Tacoma. However, some of the wildest images are real. I have known five of the six crows. I saw the coyote, the opossum, the sandwich maker, the machete girl, and even the maternal doppelgänger.

Freya's tattoo is inspired by the amazing otherworldly artwork of Erika Rier.

To Shana, this book and any other books are always for you first.

ABOUT THE AUTHOR

James Osmer lives in Tacoma, Washington with his lovely wife Shana and their dog Kinsale, who might be an escaped circus dog. In his twenties, he published over twenty poems in various small press magazines. In his thirties, he released six CDs of music as a one-man punk band on bass guitar.

In 2024, he published his first book, *Five Ways to Survive a War: The Story of How Kurt Vonnegut, Günter Grass, William Stafford, Charles Bukowski, and Richard Feynman Managed to Not Die in World War II.*

This is his first novel.